_PC_

THE FUTURE'S NOT OURS TO SEE

TO SEE

THE CARMEL SHEEHAN STORY - BOOK 2

JEAN GRAINGER

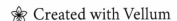

For my mother

CHAPTER 1

*C*armel Mullane caught a glimpse of herself as she crossed the glass lobby of Aashna House having just had a very productive meeting with the local horticultural club. They wanted to plant natural woodland and wild flower meadow to try to encourage some indigenous bird and insect life back to the area but the council had refused to allow them do it in the public park. She and Sharif had discussed it and now a corner of the extensive grounds of the hospice were going to be used for the purpose. Several of the residents enjoyed gardening and they would also be part of the project.

She sometimes surprised herself when she

caught her reflection. She looked like the kind of person that would have intimidated her old self, glossy hair, well cut, nice clothes, subtle but effective make-up, but more than anything, the new Carmel exuded an air of self-confidence that would have astounded her old self. She was, in every way imaginable, a new woman.

Carmel's world had been a roller coaster from that day she read the Facebook message from Sharif, standing in the dreary kitchen of Bill Sheehan's farmhouse in County Offaly, dutifully trying to be a good wife to man who couldn't care less if she lived or died. Sharif's message, out of clear blue sky told her that her entire life had been predicated on a lie, that her birth mother had not abandoned her, that she was not an unloved, unwanted child, foisted on the Irish state services. The complete opposite was true. Dolly Mullane had dedicated her life to finding her daughter, but sadly it was too late for Dolly by the time Carmel actually was found. She'd died, here at Aashna, two years before Sharif found her.

The discovery that not just Dolly loved her but that the man who was potentially her father was alive was a later revelation. Of course it didn't alleviate the pain of loss and the sense of a missed opportunity she felt on a daily basis that Dolly died before she came to Aashna, but Joe McDaid, if indeed he was her father, was alive. He didn't know of her existence. He knew nothing of what became of his girlfriend all those years ago, and it was a tale of such sadness and resentment that Carmel could hardly bear to think of it.

There were so many junctures in her life that if things had gone even slightly in another direction, it would have been so different. If Sharif had not seen CarmelIreland, her handle, on Facebook and noticed she had the same birthday as Dolly's daughter, if the nuns in the mother-and-baby home, or at Trinity, had changed her name instead of allowing her to keep the one her mother chose, if she'd ignored the message Sharif sent, if she'd chickened out of going to meet him in Dublin, and if Brian McDaid hadn't appeared in Aashna in the closing weeks of his life, then everything could have been so different.

Carmel felt the hand of her mother guiding her in ways she couldn't really verbalise, but Dolly was a strong presence in her life. Maybe Carmel was imagining it – it could well be the case, and she was sure any psychiatrist would say she was dreaming or wishing or something – but Dolly was a real and present person to her.

Carmel spoke to her often and made time each day to go to the little chapel on the grounds. It was peaceful there, and the general hubbub of the hospice didn't reach it. It was a place for reflection, for quiet time, for serenity.

Joe McDaid was never far from her thoughts as she tried to extrapolate into a future she couldn't imagine. Round and round in her mind went different scenarios. Almost every fantasy began well, with her gathering the courage to seek him out. She could picture herself outside a house in Dublin, an ordinary house on an ordinary road but inside was her father. Maybe. The fantasy always started with Carmel being brave and determined, and sometimes he was pleased at first. But then after she told him the story that Brian shared with her, he might break down, or get angry and not believe her, or perhaps he did believe her but wanted nothing to do with her. Almost inevitably it ended badly.

Since Brian's death, several nights she'd woken in tears, only to take a moment to realise where she was, in Aashna, in her and Sharif's apartment, in bed with his arms around her, soothing her.

Sharif was right – the best thing to do was just allow herself time to get used to the idea that her father might still be out there. Every time she thought about making contact with Joe McDaid, she gave up. She vacillated between thinking that her life was better than it ever was, that she should leave well enough alone, to wanting to pick up the phone and ring him.

Brian, Joe's brother and long-standing friend of Dolly's, was dead, taking with him her only tangible link to her father's family.

The arrangements for Brian's funeral had clicked into motion effortlessly, as they did on an almost daily basis in Aashna House. The whole process in England took far longer than in Ireland, where people were buried within three to four days of their death. In England it could be weeks unless there was a religious reason to do it quickly.

She'd been to hundreds of funerals in Ballyshanley – even the most tenuous connection meant one attended the funeral – and they were generally huge affairs. It was different in England, but each tradition was represented and respected and every effort was made to give everyone a fitting send-off. That was a duty often falling to Nadia, to talk with the patient and families before the death to determine what arrangements they would like. She was wonderful at it, and it ensured there was rarely a conflict after someone died as to how their passing should be marked.

Carmel recalled the night Brian died, how she felt like she had a duty to him; she'd never felt that with anyone before.

'Will I call Tim?' she'd asked as she entered the little office where Sharif was recording the details of Brian's death.

'Sure. He's expecting it, but it's still a shock.'

Carmel scrolled through her phone for the number. Then she stopped. 'You know, Sharif, I think I might just take a taxi over there, tell him in person. I know we don't normally do that, but I'd like to. Is that OK?'

He looked up. 'I'm sure he'd appreciate that. You can bring him back here with you, and we can make whatever arrangements he wants. Brian asked me to inform his family back in Ireland, but it's still very early. Given the circumstances, I don't know how much they know about his and Tim's relationship. I think we can give Tim some time before involving the extended family. It's 4:30 a.m. now, so I'll call them around eight. A few hours either way won't make any difference.'

Carmel rang Tim's mobile once the taxi dropped her outside the door.

'Hello?' Tim was instantly alert.

'Tim, it's Carmel. I'm outside your house.'

'Oh...oh, right...I see...' He seemed flustered. 'I'll be right down.'

She waited and, after a few moments, saw his shadow approach the door. He opened it and she stepped inside. He was dressed in pyjamas and a brown checked robe and slippers. No words were necessary.

He just looked at her and she nodded slightly. Tim's hand went to his face as he tried to process the news that the man he had loved for nearly decades was gone. Carmel put her arms around him, and he allowed her to comfort him. Silent tears flowed as they stood there in the hall.

'He was so peaceful, no pain at all. And at the end, he smiled so happily, Tim. He called Dolly, and his mother – I think he saw them...'

Tim released himself gently from her embrace. 'I'm glad. They were as thick as thieves, that pair, always laughing or conspiring about something. And he adored his mother. He told me that he filled you in on the story. It was their only point of argument, him and Dolly – he wanted to tell his brother so badly.'

'He did.'

They walked through to the lovely bright kitchen and Tim asked, 'Will we have a cup of tea?'

'We're Irish – it's what we do, isn't it?' She smiled.

Tim busied himself with the kettle and getting cups while she chatted. She had seen enough in the time she'd been at Aashna to know grief had many forms. No two people reacted to the death of a loved one in the same way. Sharif always allowed people the time and space to respond as they wanted, so she tried to do the same.

Tim sighed. 'I can't believe he's gone. I know that sounds stupid, as he was in a hospice and sick for so long, but I just...' His shoulders shook and Carmel went to him. She took the teapot from him and put her arms around him once more. Her kindness seemed to open the floodgates. She just stood there, letting him cry.

* * *

BRIAN WAS LAID out in the little chapel of rest in Aashna. Carmel strolled there to sit with him in the silence. His family were presumably coming from Ireland, though she had no idea of the details yet. They were her family too, it would seem, and the thought of it produced a myriad of conflicting emotions: curiosity, trepidation, excitement, terror, the whole gamut. They would arrive shortly and then she would withdraw, but for now it was nice to have the time. In the days since Brian's passing, Tim had seemed not just grief-stricken but on edge as well.

Standing beside Brian's open coffin, she hoped the sense that she got in the room when he died, that he'd seen the faces of people he loved, was what really happened. She believed in that, and she'd read of it being an international phenomenon, across all cultures, nationalities, ages and eras. When she saw the pain and the deep lines on Brian's face caused by the cancer almost smooth out, she felt such a strong sensation that he was happy to go and that he wasn't alone.

'Carmel.'

She started, snapping out of her reverie to find Sharif at her shoulder.

'Can you come home for a while?'

She smiled. She loved the way he called their little apartment home. 'Sure. Is everything OK?' She walked beside him across the butter- and gold-coloured pebbles surrounding the chapel.

'Yes, I just wanted to see you, have some time.

It's been so busy lately, and you've been arranging the programme and everything with Brian. I just miss you.' He took her hand as they approached the front door.

She stood on her tiptoes to kiss him as he put the key in the lock. 'I love you, Sharif Khan, really, really love you.'

'Of course you do – I'm fabulous.' He grinned as she swatted him on the bum.

Putting the kettle on while she opened some post that was on the mat, he said, 'There was one thing I wanted to talk to you about.'

'Go on...' She was worried.

'Well, in Brian's living will – you know, the thing people can write before they die outlining their preferences – he just asked that there be a simple Mass, no big fuss, and that his brothers and sisters be informed. He has two sisters and two brothers living, I believe, so as you know, we have contacted them, made them aware of his death, and they are going to come over for the funeral, all four of them.' She could see he was wary of telling her.

'But shouldn't Tim be doing that?' She was surprised that the job had fallen to Sharif.

'Well, the thing is, I don't think Brian's family knew he was gay.'

Carmel nodded; it made sense now, the way they were together, so united but so private. It also explained why Tim was so reticent about coming to Aashna now; he was probably afraid of running into one of Brian's family. 'I see. Poor Tim. He can't even be seen to grieve properly. It's a hard situation.'

'Well, yes, it is, but it's their choice, so we just have to do what Brian wanted. I'm sure he and Tim talked about it, so...' He shrugged.

'You didn't say anything to them about me or Dolly or...'

'Of course not.' He led her to the sofa. 'That's your story to tell, and whether you decide to tell it or not is up to you. I just wanted you to know they are coming here on Tuesday. I didn't want it to come as a shock.'

'OK... I suppose I guessed that would be the case.' She didn't know what to say. Joe McDaid, Dolly's boyfriend and possibly her father, was coming. 'Do I have to see them?'

Sharif smiled. 'Carmel, you're forty years old – you don't *have* to do anything. You don't have to go to anything you don't want to. And if you want to go to Brian's funeral as a member of Aashna House staff and not ever indicate to his family that your connection is anything more than that, then of course that's what you must do. Or if you want to tell them who you are and who your mother was, then that's fine too. Whatever you wish is fine. I'll be by your side all the time – you'll be safe.'

His voice was so gentle. He understood her insecurities. Growing up in an institution, however benign, didn't, she'd learned, equip one very well for the real world. She was so used to being told what to do and when to do it, first at Trinity House and then all those years with Bill and Julia, that she doubted the power of her own judgement. Sharif recognised that and was gently coaxing her into a life where she was the captain of her own ship.

'OK…thanks. I don't know what is for the best. I mean, they're grieving their brother and they won't need me barging in on top of them.'

'Well, if you're unsure, then why not just see how it all goes? Maybe it will come out naturally or maybe it won't. Either way, you've got me and everyone here as backup. You are not alone.'

'Maybe I should make myself scarce. I mean, it's not really my place anyway to be there. We are related, but not in any way that his family would want to know about…'

'Carmel, you work here. Of course you can

take some holidays if you like. I'm not saying it as the boss, but you have every right to be there as a member of Aashna House staff. If it helps, I spoke to his sister and she seemed very nice. She explained that Brian didn't tell them he was ill. When I asked him about family visits a few weeks ago, he told me he didn't want them fussing. His sister Maggie seemed to want me to understand that they hadn't just abandoned him. Apparently, every time they would suggest visiting, he'd say he was away or busy, and they couldn't understand why he had rejected them. Joe especially was very hurt because they were always close. Brian texted and emailed and all of that, and he went back to Dublin before the cancer got too bad, but he wouldn't allow them to visit him here. Maggie and I had a really long chat and I never mentioned what Brian said, obviously. But I think the burden of knowing what he knew about Dolly and not being able to reveal it to his brother was hard for him to bear, but he made a promise to your mother and was determined to keep it.'

Carmel nodded. She admired Brian for his loyalty to Dolly, but her heart went out to the rest of his family. She didn't know, of course, but they sounded nice and it must have been hard for them to hear he'd died and had never contacted them to say goodbye. She could never understand it when she heard of families falling out; if she'd had a family of her own, she would have loved them, but maybe that was just an overly romantic view of things.

CHAPTER 2

*C*armel lit a candle in the living room of their sunny apartment and sat down, back straight and eyes open, then took a deep breath. She exhaled and tried to still her thoughts. Today was the day of the funeral, and she was still undecided whether to go. Maggie, Brian's sister, and her husband, Dominic, had arrived from Ireland with the rest of the family the previous afternoon and checked into a local hotel. They came and spoke to Sharif and the undertaker in the evening about the arrangements, but Carmel stayed in their apartment. Just knowing that members of the McDaid family were on the grounds of Aashna was enough to make her anxious.

She tried to focus on her breath. If ever she needed direction, it was now. Part of her wanted to rush out, meet Joe, tell him who she was and ask him if he would consider a DNA test to see if he was her father. But a bigger part of her was governed by fear. She tried to analyse it – fear of what? The answer was clear: fear of rejection. What if he told her to get lost, or worse still, resented her intrusion in his grief for his brother? And all of that was leaving aside the whole business of what his father did to Dolly. She tried to focus on the future, to leave the past where it belonged, but she thought back to Brian's deathbed revelations of how Joe's father was so intent on hurting his son, how he felt such depths of hatred for his own boy that he hurt the person Joe loved the most – Dolly. She tried so hard not to run a grotesque film in her head of a young woman, happily walking home from work one winter's evening, full of excitement at the prospect of a marriage proposal from the lad she loved, only to find herself dragged into some undergrowth and raped by the man who would have been her father-in-law. And Carmel might be the product of that violent attack. She wanted to believe that it wasn't true, that she was conceived in love, but it was all so complicated. She knew from the way

Brian explained it that nobody in the McDaid family was under any illusion about what kind of man their father was, but he was dead now. How would they react to a total stranger showing up, raking over old ground, bringing all those painful memories to the surface once more? Or perhaps with time they had come to forgive him for being a terrible father, a violent husband, and her intruding on their lives, claiming to be a part of their family would be rejected out of hand. She couldn't blame them. Every time she thought she had the guts to face them all, she was crushed by an icy wave of dread crashing over her head once again.

She listened to the guided meditation for calm, the soothing voice on the sound system encouraging her to fill her senses with serenity, to picture herself walking by the ocean, to see herself barefoot, on the beach, the warm waves lapping around her feet, the sun on her face, breathing in the warm salty air. Normally it worked, but not today; she was too wound up. Her mouth was dry, her heart was pounding, and there was a cold prickle of sweat between her shoulder blades. She switched the meditation off and checked her watch; it was almost time.

In the small hours of the morning when there

was no possibility of sleep, she had decided to take Sharif's advice to just go as a member of the staff and see what happened.

She was dressed in black trousers, black ankle boots and a cream shirt, and her blonde hair was brushed till it shone. She thought she should wear some make-up; her eyes had dark circles beneath them from lack of sleep. She applied some concealer and foundation but didn't risk anything else. Before she could start to overthink it again and dredge up all the associated fears, she grabbed her bag and went out the door.

Approaching the chapel, she almost fled, but forced herself to walk on. Sharif had offered to accompany her, but she needed to do this on her own. In general he didn't attend funerals; if he were to start that process, he would get nothing done and some family would be bound to be insulted if he missed their loved one's memorial service. So he made time for each family after a patient's death and left it at that.

She hoped her appearance was just neutral. In Ballyshanley, she used to blend seamlessly into the background with her boring clothes and mousy-brown hair, but less so now. Her blonde hair had been restored, and she was aware for the first time in her life of admiring glances from men. But she only had eyes for one. Perhaps she should have taken him up on the offer to go with her. Suddenly she longed for Sharif's tall, solid presence. He was so unusual looking, with his dark almond-shaped eyes that looked like they were ringed in kohl, skin the colour of caramel and silver hair, that nobody would take a second look at her.

The beautiful engagement ring he'd given her was back in the apartment; she felt it was too flashy for a funeral.

She debated stopping and introducing herself to the group chatting quietly outside the chapel, but she lost courage, so she just continued inside and took a seat at the back. Only the undertaker and the priest were inside preparing for the ceremony, and the coffin was at the top of the chapel. In Ireland it was traditional for the body to be taken from the house or hospital by hearse and driven to the church, where the deceased would lie overnight, but things were done differently here. She hoped the undertaker was aware of the cultural and procedural differences between the countries and that someone had explained it to the McDaids. She almost smiled at the sense of protectiveness she felt for that family, though to them she was just Aashna staff.

The music began to play, and Brian's family slowly walked in. Carmel instantly recognised the hymn; it was 'Our Lady of Knock'. She'd always loved that one as a child. The lyrics told the story of a group of poor people, children included, who saw an apparition of the Virgin Mary on the gable wall of the church in 1879. The idea that such things happened in Lourdes or Garabandal or Fatima was one thing, but that Our Lady chose a small village in County Mayo was always a source of pride to her young self. She never doubted the validity of the testimonies of those present at the time, though she wasn't sure now. She'd never been to County Mayo, but it warmed her to think such a place existed in Ireland.

Being confronted with Ireland and the Irish again was something she'd have to steel herself for. To her, she now realised, England meant a safe haven, a place of refuge from the sadness of the past. Though she loved to hear the Irish accents and think about aspects of life that were unique to her native country, she knew that she had no wish to ever return. The Carmel Murphy, then Sheehan, that scared child, then woman, who endured life back there no longer existed and would never return, not if Carmel could help it.

The family took their seats at the top of the small chapel, all sitting on the front pew, and Carmel fixed her gaze on Brian's sisters and brothers as they passed. They looked like any other family, she supposed. The two sisters were polar opposites, one tall and slim and elegant, the other short and heavyset. The men were tall, both grey-haired; one had blue eyes, the other grey. Which one was Joe, she wondered. Behind them were close to twenty other people – wives, husbands and children, she assumed. She smiled at how Irish they all looked; even the number of people attending was Irish. She had been saddened at first when she came to England to note how few people went to funerals. She had explained to Zane and Ivy that funerals were as big as weddings in Ireland, bigger often because no invitations were issued. They'd laughed when she told them that back in Ireland they say the only difference between a wedding and a funeral is one less drunk.

Anyone who had even the most tenuous of connections to the departed went to a local funeral, and those who were connected to the family of the person too. Colleagues, old school friends of the deceased's grandchildren, almost everyone in the town or village if it was in the country went. Back in Ballyshanley, she and Bill went to every single removal or funeral in the whole town. It would have been considered the height of disrespect not to. The family was propped up emotionally by their community for a long while afterwards, food was delivered, the house became a kind of open house, and people came and went to pay their respects, eat and drink. The body was almost always laid out in the sitting room, and people would come by the coffin for a final goodbye, often kissing the person's head. Carmel had explained that in the café one day, and people were astounded. Death here in England was a private thing.

'But what about children and so on?' Ivanka had asked, fascinated.

'What about them?' Carmel was confused.

'Well, if the body is lying there and everyone mills around it, who takes care of the children?'

Carmel smiled. 'They are there too. The Irish don't have a weirdness about death that seems to persist here. Dead bodies are part of life, and little children would always see their dead people lying in their coffins. And unless the death was tragic or of someone young, there's a kind of happy atmosphere. It's hard to describe, but in Ireland a funeral really is a celebration. People stand around telling stories, eating and drinking and remembering. If it's summertime, the people gather outside too, and loud bursts of raucous laughter or even a sing-song wouldn't be unheard of.'

She found to her astonishment that her new friends were fascinated with every aspect of life in the next island over; very few British people had ever visited Ireland. Because emigration was so much a part of the Irish story, people going to England for work was commonplace, but the traffic across the Irish Sea seemed distinctly one way.

She'd told them about how beautiful Ireland was, how steeped in history and culture. And when Zane suggested they all go for a long weekend to Dublin, she'd gone along with it, but she knew nothing would ever drag her back there again.

CHAPTER 3

*W*hen the family were settled, she felt someone slide into the seat behind her. She turned slightly and realised it was Tim.

Carmel's heart went out to the McDaid family; they were like fish out of water over here. Back at home, because there was a protocol, a way of doing death, everyone knew what to do. In Ireland, it was as if when someone died, a switch got flicked and the age-old process just cranked into action. Each person knew his or her part, and people were comforted by that. Over here, in this strange country, the McDaids were lost.

Father Watson, the local Catholic priest, said the funeral Mass, and the familiar words soothed

Carmel's frantic spirit. She felt such a barrage of emotions as she sat there – fear, guilt at not focusing properly on Brian, comfort from the words of the familiar liturgy, all underpinned by a longing for her mother. Brian's nephew Daniel gave a short but heartfelt eulogy of a loving uncle, someone the family loved to have come for a visit. He was always laden down with treats and toys for his many nieces and nephews. There was an air of levity to the proceedings laced in with the sadness of the loss. Brian had been very well loved, it was clear. The hymns were traditional, Brian's own choice, and played on the elaborate sound system in the church. The priest blessed the coffin, sprinkling it with holy water as he intoned the prayers of death.

'Into your hands we commend our brother Brian. Eternal rest grant unto him, O Lord, and may perpetual light shine on him forever. May he rest in peace.'

The Mass ended, and the men in the family, Brian's two brothers in front, nephews behind, shouldered Brian's coffin out to the hearse. As they passed, the women were silently weeping, the men stony-faced. Of the two brothers, one was slightly taller, so she assumed him to be Joe. His face was set in a mask of grief, and as he passed her seat, she tried to find some trace of herself in his features. The only photo she had, taken all those years ago on Dollymount Strand, showed him as towering over Dolly.

Outside in the sunshine, Carmel felt awkward and stood with Tim, slipping her arm through his. She knew he was stoic, but this was killing him. The nephew who gave the eulogy approached them.

'Em...I don't know who ye are, but obviously my uncle meant something to you both, so we'd be happy to have you come with us to the crematorium, and afterwards to the hotel for a bit of lunch?'

Tim recovered first, though he sounded more than a little strangled. 'Thank you, that's very kind. We'd love to.'

Carmel squeezed his arm in a gesture of solidarity. This was his life partner and yet the last act of Brian's life had Tim playing a bit part. It was so hard.

The cremation was short. Father Watson said a few more prayers, and the family looked awkward. Cremation was very rare in Ireland, and Carmel guessed it was their first time attending one. The whole ceremony went by in a blur. Thoughts of introducing herself to Brian's family,

Joe in particular, were petrifying. Should she just say she worked at Aashna House and, since she was Irish, felt she should go? Or should she admit that she and Brian had been friends? Or could she just let Tim introduce himself and let them assume she was something to do with him? To her shame, she wasn't thinking about Brian at all as his coffin slid behind the screen; she was panicking about how to get out of the situation. All the calming, mindful thoughts of that morning were gone and in their place was terror.

'Have you ever met any of them?' Carmel whispered to Tim as the family huddled together around the door of the crematorium.

'Never. Brian didn't want them to know about us. He wanted to protect me and my life, so he lived a lie all these years for me. By the time it was OK for us to say what we meant to each other, it was too late, too much time had passed, too much had been left unsaid, too many lies told. So when he went home, he went alone. Any time he had a visitor from Ireland, which was rare, I made myself scarce. It must seem odd to someone of your generation, as everyone is so open nowadays, but it just wasn't like that in our day. And well, we're bad with change – at least we were. It's just me now, I suppose.'

Carmel gave a wry grin. 'I didn't have the liberal upbringing you imagine I had, Tim, nothing like it, so I totally understand.'

Daniel approached them, and it took Carmel everything she had to stay on the spot, as the urge to flee was so strong.

'So ye'll come down to the hotel, will ye? The Davenport it's called. We can do proper introductions there. We've a few taxis coming, so ye can jump in with us or if ye have yer own car?' He was a handsome young man, and his open, honest face drew a smile from Carmel.

'Yes, we have a car. We'll see you there.' Tim squeezed Carmel's arm to his body, murmuring into her ear as they made their way to the car park. 'We're going to need to stick together on this one, my dear.'

'Carmel!'

She turned to see Sharif striding towards her.

'Hello, Tim.' Sharif shook the other man's hand; they hadn't met since Brian died. 'I'm so sorry for your loss.'

Tim nodded. 'I didn't know it would be that night. I left earlier than usual, and I had a hospital appointment myself early the next morning, and I...'

Carmel held his arm as the emotion choked him.

'I...I wanted to be with him, but he said he didn't want me to remember him like that, so we agreed...'

'He wasn't alone. Carmel was with him, and so was I. He had a very peaceful death.' Sharif was soothing.

'He wrote me a letter and put it in a box, to be opened when he died, along with some things that were of sentimental value to us, little souvenirs and things, but the letter... He never was a very publicly effusive man. Neither am I – we weren't brought up that way. Maybe people nowadays would say we were a bit stuffy or formal or whatever, but it worked for us. But this letter, it was everything we felt but never said. He wrote it all. I would have liked the chance to tell him I felt the same.' Tim struggled to maintain his composure.

'He knew.' Carmel was sure of it.

'So where are you going now?' Sharif asked gently.

'To the hotel, the Davenport. The family have invited us for lunch.' Carmel knew the dread that she felt was clearly visible on her face.

'Do they know – the family, I mean –who you,

or Tim for that matter, do they know who you are?' Concern furrowed his smooth forehead.

'No. No, they don't have a clue who either of us is.' Carmel chewed her lip, a habit she'd had since childhood.

Tim recovered and gave a lopsided grin. 'We're debating which of us should explain first.'

'Do you want me to come with you?' Sharif was talking directly to Carmel now. 'Would it help?'

'But your patients, they need you this afternoon surely...' Carmel desperately wanted him there but felt guilty taking him away.

'Well, I didn't know how today was going to go, so I got a locum in anyway, Dr Alexander. The patients are used to her as she often covers for me, so I'm free to go with you if it would help. But if you'd rather do this alone, then I understand, of course.'

She looked up at him, shielding her eyes from the bright sun. 'I'd love you to come.'

CHAPTER 4

Sharif drove them all, as Tim was too shaken. They found a parking space and Carmel and Tim got out, leaving Sharif to take a phone call about a patient.

'What are you going to say?' Tim sounded as scared she was.

'I don't know. I can't decide. How about you?'

'Not the truth anyway, that's for sure. Just that we were friends, he was my lodger, something like that, I suppose.' The sadness and grief at not just losing the love of his life but also having to deny the importance of their relationship was really hurting him – it was plain for anyone to see.

'OK, are we ready?' Sharif caught up with

them and gently put his hand on the small of Carmel's back.

'Yes. Well, no, actually, not at all ready, but if we are going to do this...'

Before they had a chance to compose themselves, Brian's sisters approached them.

'Hello, Dr Khan. It's very good of you to come. I'm Maggie and this is my sister, Orla. Brian's brothers Colm and Joe are inside, along with some of our kids. Daniel said you two were friends of Brian's?' Her open face radiated friendliness and welcome even in the midst of her obvious grief at the loss of her brother.

'Yes, Tim O'Flaherty. Brian used to live in my house.' Tim extended a hand and Maggie took it warmly. She was short with iron-grey hair and was what Julia would have called 'a victim of middle-age spread', a fate that was never likely to befall the angular Julia. Maggie was dressed all in black, but Carmel got the impression she was uncomfortable in the dress, jacket and tights. Orla was the opposite, very glamorous, with expensively cut and highlighted hair and a well-cut trouser suit. She seemed more wary than her sister, despite the smile. Both women looked expectantly at Carmel.

'I'm Carmel.' She didn't want to use her mother's surname in case they recognised it, but she couldn't bring herself to use the name 'Carmel Sheehan' one more time. 'I work at Aashna House, and I got to know Brian there, what with us both being Irish,' she finished in a rush, desperate to get the words out.

'You look very familiar. I can't place from where, but I feel as though I know you from somewhere.' Orla's brow furrowed. 'I've thought it since I saw you in the chapel. And you're Irish. Where did you go to school? Maybe we were in the same one?'

'I…ah…I went to school in Dublin, city centre, but Brian said you were from Kilmainham – didn't you go there?' Carmel was anxious to deflect this line of questioning.

'Yes, we went to Inchicore National School and then to St Jarlath's in Ballyfermot.' Orla was clearly racking her brain.

'Well, I didn't go to either of those. I think I just have one of those faces – people are always saying I remind them of someone.' Carmel's laugh sounded fake even to her own ears.

Sensing her discomfort, Sharif interrupted. 'Shall we go in?'

Both Maggie and Orla responded instantly to his charm and turned towards him like sunflowers. 'Of course, Dr Khan.' Maggie recovered enough to lead the little group in.

'Sharif, please.' He smiled as he held the door open for the three ladies. Carmel caught his eye and gave him a look of thanks.

The introductions were made, and nobody seemed to bat an eyelid at the three extra for lunch. The chat was lively, and the family even burst into spontaneous laughter on occasion. Despite their pain and genuine loneliness for their brother and uncle, the lunch really was a celebration of a life well lived.

After the main course and after the waitresses took tea and coffee orders, Joe stood up and dinged his spoon off his wine glass and the family settled down. Carmel's mouth went dry and she was transfixed. Was this man her father? He was tall, with an athletic build and grey hair cut short. She thought he looked in good shape for a man of sixty-plus years. His blue eyes were exactly the same colour as hers; Dolly's eyes were hazel.

He waited until everyone was silent and then spoke. His voice was gentle, and he had a real Dublin accent, just like Brian had. 'Family and friends of my late brother Brian, I just wanted to say a few words. As most of you know, burying our brother Kevin two years ago was a very low time for all of us, and we are really happy that Kevin Junior and Ciara can be here with us – it means a lot. Brian was the eldest of the McDaids, and in lots of ways, more ways than he should have been actually, he was the father figure. He was kind and always had time for any one of us, no matter what we ever needed. There was a time when I was a young man that I thought my heart would break, but it was Brian who held me together. When Mammy died, when Kevin was taken from us so early, when the engagements happened or babies were born, the first thing we did was tell Brian. When he left Ireland, it left a huge hole in all our hearts, but we were glad to see he had a happy life over here. He came home often, laden down with presents every time, and he was always welcome. He texted and emailed us all the time, so he never felt too far away.' Joe swallowed, composing himself to continue. Carmel could feel the room willing him on.

'I want, on behalf of the McDaid family, to extend a warm welcome to Dr Khan, who is with us here today, and to whom we all owe a great debt. He looked after Brian in the closing weeks of his life. He respected his wishes and maintained his dignity, while at the same time giving him the benefit of expert care. Brian emailed me a week ago and told me all about you, Doctor, how he never suffered, physically or mentally, and for that, Dr Khan, we are so grateful.'

Sharif nodded and smiled, and Carmel squeezed his hand under the table. She knew he wasn't comfortable with accolades; he was a true doctor, just wanting to help people.

'Welcome as well to his fiancée, Carmel, who is a Paddy the same as ourselves.'

There was a ripple of laughter.

'I understand that you had some nice chats with Brian in his last days, and we are glad that he had someone from home to talk to. Finally, we want to say thank you and welcome to Tim O'Flaherty, who was a great friend to Brian during all his years over here. Tim, there's a bed for you in Dublin any time you like.'

Several heads nodded and smiles were directed at Tim, making him blush.

Joe went on. 'Brian never told us how ill he was and he didn't encourage visitors, but we never doubted what we meant to him, and I pray that he knew how much he meant to us too. So please, raise your glasses to Brian McDaid, always loved and never forgotten.'

'To Brian,' the gathered crowd chorused, and glasses clinked.

Carmel held Tim's eye as their water glasses tapped.

Joe sat down to thunderous applause. Then Daniel stood up. 'Hip hip...'

The gathered group answered, 'Hurrah!' And once again the lunch became a jovial affair.

Carmel chatted with one of Brian's nieces, Colm's daughter Aisling. She was funny and refreshing, telling stories of the shenanigans of her uncles and aunts when they all got together. They sounded like such a happy family, and the cousins were clearly all good friends. Carmel wondered what it would be like to grow up like that, so happy and loved and surrounded by your people, to know that you were part of something.

Tim, sitting on her right, just observed the whole family, the pain of loss and grief hidden behind his eyes and his smile.

'How are you bearing up?' Aisling had popped to the bathroom, so Carmel had a chance to speak to him quietly.

'OK. You know...they loved him, of course they did, but in an old-uncle-over-in-England kind of way, not...'

'Not the way you did.' She placed her hand on his. 'I know. It must be so hard behaving like an outsider when you're, in fact, the chief mourner.'

Tim nodded, his mouth set in a hard line, trying to hold it together. 'I think I'll go, actually. Thanks for today.' He pushed his chair back, and without a word to anyone, he was gone.

Sharif caught her eye. He read her glance correctly, that she too had had enough and wanted to go. He made his farewells and helped Carmel into her coat.

'Thanks for having us. It was so lovely to meet you all. And I'm sure wherever Brian is now, he's looking down and smiling,' Carmel managed to say, and with waves and warm handshakes, she took her leave of the McDaids. She hadn't spoken to Joe at all, deliberately placing herself at the other end of the table.

As they made their way across the car park, they spotted Tim waiting on a cab. They'd forgotten he had come to the hotel with them; his car was back at the crematorium.

'Tim,' Carmel called, 'come with us. We'll take you back to your car.'

He didn't answer, just raised his hand, suggesting he was fine. Carmel and Sharif walked over to him. He looked as if he was just about holding it together, but when Carmel linked his arm, suddenly tears poured down his lined and age-spotted face. Without a word, they led him to the car and Carmel got in the back with him. Sharif drove, and she held Tim's hand as he wept.

'He was my world. What am I supposed to do now? Everyone else will be a bit sad, but they'll go back to their lives. But...Brian was my life. Without him, I just don't know how to be, what to do.'

Carmel held his hand and said nothing. Tim just needed to talk, to articulate the pain. She wished she could ease it for him, but there was no way around grief, just through it. The familiar streets passed by in a blur.

Once they were back at the crematorium, it didn't feel right just to let him go off on his own, back to the home he'd shared with Brian for so many years. 'Would you like to go for a cup of tea? Or something stronger?' she asked.

'THANKS. You've both been so kind – I really appreciate it. But no, I think I'll just go home. It's been a long day, and I just want to get into bed and be alone with my thoughts. I hope you understand?'

'Of course we do,' Sharif reassured him. 'It has been a really hard day for you, made harder by the fact that you couldn't grieve properly. But,

Tim, celebrating a life, remembering, having those precious memories, they don't mean much today, but they will in time become important, and all of this today will be irrelevant.'

Sharif had a way of speaking to the bereaved that constantly impressed Carmel. It was as if he knew what to say. He wasn't at all morose or dreary, quite the opposite actually. He was full of fun, but he had a deep compassion and understanding of the human condition.

They saw Tim to his car, waved him off and headed home to Aashna. Carmel longed for a soak in the bath, a gin and tonic and an early night. It had been a gruelling day, and even though the McDaid family had no idea who she really was, she still felt the burden of the knowledge she had, thanks to Brian, weighing heavily on her. Maybe she should have said something, but it wasn't the right time.

She sat heavily on the couch, kicking off her shoes and examining a blister on the sole of her foot caused by the new shoes she'd bought for the occasion. Maybe there would never be a right time. She was too tired and wrung out to even think about it any more.

Sharif had some calls to make and needed to do his evening rounds, but before he left, he ran her a bath, lit a candle for her in the bathroom and made her a drink. 'Now you relax there, listen to some music and try to let the strain of the day melt away. I'll be about an hour. Will I bring you something from the kitchen? Are you hungry?' He was in front of her, gin and tonic in hand.

'How on earth did I get you?' She took the drink and put her hand on the side of his face. He turned his face and kissed her palm. 'Seriously, Sharif, I don't know how I'd have got through today without you. Thank you.'

'We're a team now, Carmel. Together, there is nothing we can't do. Now, relax, have a soak, and I'll be back soon.'

She watched his departing back as he left the apartment, his mind now on those people who needed him. She tried to imagine Bill ever doing anything thoughtful for anyone.

So many times, she'd started a letter to Bill, but it always sounded crazy. She and Bill never spoke and had no relationship, and to try to talk to him as her husband, as someone she should be close to, felt so uncomfortable that she ended up throwing all her efforts in the bin. In the end, their break-up had many of the characteristics of their marriage – a cold, empty nothingness, with no explanation or attempt to soothe from either side.

She went into the bedroom to undress, when there was a knock on the door. Her heart sank. It was probably Nadia, calling to see how she'd got on, or Zane with some Grindr crisis that could only be solved by Chardonnay and lots of analysis. He was forever falling in love with fit young men he met on the gay dating app, but he seemed to fall out of love too with remarkable haste. Normally, she would have been thrilled to see either of them, but she was so drained she couldn't face company. She just stood in the bedroom and hoped the person would go away. They might assume she was in bed already if she drew the curtains.

The knocking was insistent, however, and she knew she'd have to go out and answer the door. She threw her pyjamas and dressing gown on and stuck her feet in her furry mule slippers and went out, determined to make her excuses.

The bubble glass meant she couldn't make out who was there, but it certainly wasn't ebony-skinned Zane nor the tiny Nadia. She opened the door.

CHAPTER 5

'Joe.' His name almost caught in Carmel's throat.

'I'm sorry for calling unannounced, but...can I come in?' He looked shaken and drawn.

'Er...yes...of course...come in. Sharif isn't here if it's him you want to see – he's doing his rounds over at the main building...' She knew she was babbling, but this was just too close for comfort.

'It was you I wanted to see, Carmel.' His strong Dublin accent took her back to her days in Trinity House.

'Oh...oh, right. Em...sure... Em...what can I do for you?'

'You can tell me how someone the living spit of Dolly Mullane ended up at my brother's funeral for a start.'

Carmel felt the colour drain from her face. Her insides turned to ice water, and a cold sweat prickled her skin. She walked in a daze through to the sofa and invited him to sit down.

'No thanks,' he said. 'Look, I'm sorry for barging in, but there's no point in denying it. The minute I saw you, I knew. Don't ask me how it happened, but you're something to Dolly Mullane – I'd put my life on it. Am I right? Brian had something to do with it...I know that much. Something he said a few months ago, about Dolly, I don't know. He never let on, but I had a feeling always that he knew something about what became of her. And then you show up...'

'Would you like a drink?' Her voice sounded stronger than she felt. She needed to play for time, think how she was going to handle this.

'By the look on your face, I think I'm going to need one.' He tried to crack a small smile.

She made herself another gin and tonic and made one for Joe as well.

'So am I right? Are you related to Dolly?' he asked as she handed him the drink.

There was no point in lying, but Carmel had

no idea where to begin. She took a deep breath and tried to steady herself. Eventually she spoke. 'Yes, Dolly was my birth mother.'

'What do you mean, "birth mother"?'

'Well, I never met her. She died before Sharif found me.' Seeing his confusion, she knew she had to tell him the story from the beginning, leaving nothing out. 'You'll want to sit down. It's a long story,' she said.

Joe sat on the couch. She sat opposite him in the armchair and tried to compose her thoughts. There had been enough secrets and lies; now was the time for truth. Filling in the blanks in the story between Brian's, Nadia's and Sharif's recollections of Dolly's life, she told Joe everything she knew. His face when she told him about his father's attack and Dolly's subsequent pregnancy almost broke her heart. The raw agony – it was as if it had happened yesterday.

He allowed her to tell her story, everything about his father and the ban on her adoption, and when she was finished, they sat in silence.

'So my father was your father?' He seemingly could barely get the words out.

This was it, the moment when she told him. Suddenly it all felt like too much. What if he rejected it? Told her she was lying? Could she cope with him refusing to accept responsibility for her? She wished Sharif were there. Taking a deep breath, she blurted it out. 'Possibly, or it might be you. Dolly didn't know. It could have been either of you, but your father threatened her, and so she left. She couldn't tell you, because if she did, your father said that you'd try to kill him and that you'd end up in prison, and her father would have the scandal of that to add to his pregnant daughter. So she did the only thing she could. Your father put her in the home for unmarried mothers run by the nuns. And as I say, I was raised in an orphanage.'

'And you?' It was clear he could barely bring himself to ask. 'Did they hurt you?'

'No. Not like abuse or anything. It was OK.'

'And the years since then? Have you been here all this time?' He was struggling, she could see.

She told him all about Bill and his proposal, and Joe's jaw tightened. They sat in silence for a long minute, Joe trying to absorb what he'd heard, Carmel trying to see his reaction. Rage, upset, sorrow, pity – it was all there on his face.

'I can't believe that he wouldn't let you be adopted. He was an evil man – I always knew that. He was horrible to us as kids and to our ma, and he couldn't bear us challenging him. He drove Brian away because he tried to defend me. For a year after Dolly disappeared, he'd goad me about her, saying she must have left me for a real man, all that sort of stuff. My heart was broken, it hurt so much. Brian told him to shut up one night, to leave me alone, and he made his life hell after that. If only she'd told me, or written even… I can't understand how they never said anything. Brian knew how much I suffered. He would have told her. And even if she contacted me after my father died…'

'But you were married then, had children of your own. She didn't want to upset your life, I suppose, thought she'd done enough damage.'

'But Mary – that was my late wife – she knew all about Dolly. Sure we all grew up together. I remember one night, after our son, Luke, was born, thirty-two years ago now, and Jennifer was a toddler, she says to me, "I know you'll never love me the way you loved Dolly, but is this enough? Is what we have enough for you?"' His voice betrayed the emotions going on inside. 'I told her that it was, that I loved her and the kids so much, and I was telling the truth. I really did, and we had a great marriage, but she knew… There was a big part of me that was never going to get over Dolly.'

They sat and talked for over an hour, Carmel filling in what she knew about her mother's life in England, most of which she'd learned from Nadia and Sharif, and Joe told Carmel all about growing up in Kilmainham and what Dolly was like as a child. They never mentioned his possible paternity.

'So now what do we do?' Joe said eventually, looking uncertain.

'About what?' Carmel knew exactly what he meant, but she needed to hear him say it.

'About you and me, and us figuring out if we are father and daughter or brother and sister.' The words fell between them like lead weights.

'What do you want to do?' Carmel heard herself swallow.

Joe reached over and took her hand in his, touching her for the first time. She could feel her heart thumping in her chest and was sure he could hear it too. He sighed deeply, the weight of all he'd discovered bearing down on him.

'What I want can't happen. I want to turn the clock back to the day before he attacked her. I want Dolly to have come to me forty years ago, telling me that she was expecting and that we had to get married. I'd have married her in a heartbeat. I want to have raised you as my daughter with Dolly as your mother and my wife, and maybe a few more along with you to keep you company. I want none of this to have happened. For that pathetic excuse for a man to have never laid a hand on my lovely Dolly, for you not to have had a lonely childhood with nobody to love you, for you to have never married that eejit down the country. I wish lots of things, but wishing won't change the past. As my ma was fond of saying, if wishes were horses, beggars would ride. All we have is now and the hand we've been dealt.'

So many thoughts and questions rushed through Carmel's head. Did this man want her to be his daughter? Did he want to find out? Did he wish he'd never uncovered this awful secret? Was he still in love with Dolly? Did his children know that he loved Dolly before their mother? It was too overwhelming; she needed a minute to process her thoughts.

'I want to show you something.' She got up and went to the bedroom where she kept the letters and the photos Dolly had left for her. She still looked at them every day. As she rooted in the box, she caught sight of her reflection in the mirror; she looked haggard and drawn. Then she stopped and really looked into her own eyes.

Others saw her mother there; perhaps she could too.

She spoke silently to her. *Mam, Dolly, please help us all here. I don't know what to do, what to say. You seem to be guiding me, and so far, it's been for the best, bringing me here, to Sharif and Nadia. I finally have a life of my own. But this, with Joe, I'm lost. Please, help me.*

She found the photo she was looking for and brought it to Joe. She handed it to him, and instantly she saw the flood of recognition in his eyes.

'Where did this come from? God, we look so young! We must only have been twenty or twenty-one then. I remember the day it was taken, out on Dollymount. We'd both been paid, so we went to the seaside on the bus and had chips and ice creams and swam in the freezing-cold sea. That night, we came home and Dolly's father was out. We made love for the first time then, a first for both of us.' He was clearly reminiscing out loud and looked embarrassed at the revelation. 'Sorry. TMI, I suppose, as my daughter is fond of saying.' He gave a lopsided grin.

'Please, tell me more. I'd love to hear more about you two.'

CHAPTER 6

*J*oe smiled, seemingly transfixed by Carmel's face. 'Well, if we were caught, he'd have strung me up, but Dolly was sure he was out for the night. He did catch us another night and threw me out and was raging with Dolly, but he softened in the end. He knew I was stone mad about her, and she wasn't the kind of girl that went off with this fella and that fella – she wasn't like that at all. But she and me, we had a bond since we were kids. We loved each other.' Tears welled up in his eyes, and he wiped them impatiently with the back of his hand. 'How did you get these pictures if she was dead before you came here?' he asked.

'She left them with Sharif, in case he ever

found me. Those, some jewellery and a bunch of letters. Apart from one of me as a baby, it's the only picture from her life before she came over here.' Suddenly she needed Joe to know how hard Brian had fought for him to know the truth. 'Brian and Dolly fell out, you know, though she looked after him when he got sick and visited him and all of that. But he was so angry with her. He wanted to tell you everything as soon as he stumbled across her, but she wouldn't let him. She made him swear to keep it all to himself.'

'But I don't understand why. I mean, she knew I loved her and that even after all these years, I'd want to know.' Joe was so sad; it hurt Carmel to hear the pain in his voice.

'She just felt that she'd hurt you enough, I think, that you were happy with a family of your own and that anything she said at that stage would just upset that. She just didn't ever want you to know what your father did to her, and to me – it wouldn't have helped. I'm only basing this on what Brian told me. I never met her, and I so wish that I had, even for one day.'

'I wouldn't mind a word with her myself, now that I know what I know. It's so strange for me, to be here, looking at you. I can't tell you how much you look like her. I never knew Dolly when she was your age. She was gone from me a long time by then. But I can see her in you, clear as day. Your eyes are different, though. Hers were hazel and yours are blue, like mine.'

'I know.' She wanted to ask what colour his father's eyes were, but she couldn't. 'Everyone says that I look like her. I never looked like anyone, so it's strange for me too, I can assure you. She and I are different in personality, though, based on what I've been told. She was much more outgoing than I am, much braver too probably.'

'You're remarkable. You don't seem to be angry. I'm bloody furious, and yet it was to you all of this happened, and you seem OK with it.'

Carmel didn't know how to take that. Perhaps it was a criticism, but she couldn't be sure. 'Oh, I'm not OK, nothing like it, but there's no point in harbouring anger. It would only hurt me, and those people who didn't behave as they should have, well, my being a mess wouldn't impact on them in any way, would it? I'm trying to come to terms with it all.'

Joe smiled. 'You're right, of course you are, but still. You say you're not like your mother in personality, but I think you are in some ways. She was kind of pragmatic as well. When her mother died and her father was hard to deal with, she just accepted it and tried to make the best of it. Even her life over here – she was obviously torn apart after losing you, but she tried to make the best life for herself that she could.'

They chatted easily. There was no awkwardness or wondering what to say next, and Carmel stopped fretting about his reaction to the news. As usual, Sharif was gone much longer than he'd anticipated, but Carmel was used to it and knew he'd be back when he'd got everyone settled for the night.

She heard Sharif's key in the door, and as he entered, his face registered surprise to see Joe sitting there.

'Don't worry, Sharif,' Joe said. 'I'm not in here trying to charm your fiancée.' He smiled and stood up to shake Sharif's hand.

'I should hope not.' Sharif chuckled and kissed Carmel on the cheek. 'I take it you two have been chatting?' The enquiring look he gave Carmel meant he was checking who knew what before he continued with any conversation.

'Yes. Joe knew who I was right away. Apparently I couldn't be anyone else, only Dolly Mullane's daughter. I've told him the whole story, or as much as I know anyway, everything Brian told me too, and also information about her life here from your mum and you.'

'It's quite a tale, is it not?' Sharif poured himself a glass of red wine and joined them.

'It certainly is,' Joe agreed. 'What we have to decide now is what to do next.'

The words hung in the air. All the time they'd been talking, they had both studiously avoided the question of a DNA test. From Carmel's perspective, she wanted to know, but then she wondered if she might be better off not knowing? The idea that Joe was her father, now that she'd met him properly, was such a lovely one, and the alternative was horrible. Maybe if they never found out, they could just carry on and... She stopped herself from that crazy train of thought. Of course he would want to know.

'What do you want to do, Carmel?' Joe asked gently.

'I don't know.'

He leaned over and took her hand again. It felt so natural, so comforting. 'Well, will I tell you what I think?'

She nodded, not trusting herself to speak.

'I think you're my daughter. Maybe I only think that because I want it to be the case, but I don't know, I just think you are. You have my eyes. I'd love it if you were, and I know once I explain to Jennifer and Luke, they'll welcome you with open arms. They're great and you'd love them. And if you want to do a test – and I think they can do that now fairly easily – then that's what we'll do. But if you don't, well, that's fine with me too.'

Carmel felt the reassuring weight of Sharif's hand on her shoulder, and it calmed her.

Joe went on, and his words were like a soothing balm on a raw wound. 'I want to be your dad. It's late in the day now, but even so, I can't just walk out of here and say, well, best of luck with your life, and leave it at that. It would drive me crazy. So, Carmel, the ball is in your court, as they say. I'm here, and I would love to call you my daughter and try to make up even in a small way for all the pain, but if you don't want that, well then, I'll be very sad but I'll accept it.'

He stood up to leave. 'I don't want an answer now. There's no time limit on the offer. I know this must be so overwhelming. It is for me too. So I'll leave you both to talk it over, and maybe we could meet up before I go home tomorrow night? Or if that's too soon, here's my number.' He handed her a card. 'Ring any time, or visit, whatever suits you, Carmel. No pressure.'

She stood and took a step towards him as if it were the most natural thing in the world. He wrapped his arms around her, and she laid her head against his chest. The overwhelming feeling was one of safety and peace. He kissed the top of her head and was gone.

That night, she and Sharif talked about it in bed. A part of her wanted, needed, to know the truth, and another part of her just wanted Joe to be her father and for her to be in his life. The idea that he would accept her as his, even without knowing the truth, was a testament to the kind of man he was. He was obviously worthy of the love Dolly had for him all those years ago.

After going around in conversational circles for hours, Sharif leaned up on his elbow and looked down into her face. 'Carmel, I have an idea. Say if it's a terrible one, but you've had such a harrowing few months. It must feel sometimes like you're being dragged under a sea of emotions. I was thinking, why don't we take a holiday? Take a little time out together? Just the two of us? It's been so busy since you came over here, and I'd love just to spend some time with you away from all the distractions. Just for a week maybe, somewhere sunny and calm, where we can just relax and get away from all of this. What do you think?'

She'd never had a holiday, even when she and Bill had got married. They drove home to Ballyshanley that evening, and he was out milking within half an hour of arriving at the farm. The idea of a honeymoon was never suggested. 'That would be absolutely amazing, even though our life here is a kind of endless holiday for me. But you never take a rest. Your mother was only saying last week that it was ridiculous that you never take any time off. And I must say, the idea of having you all to myself for a whole week...well, that would just be bliss.'

'Hmmm...' He kissed her neck, sending shivers of desire through her body. She had no idea that her body could react that way until he'd kissed her that very first time. 'Of course, I *am* all yours now...'

CHAPTER 7

*C*armel was on a coffee break in the bright, sunny restaurant, sitting opposite Zane and Ivanka.

'Ah, no… I mean, thank you, it's a lovely thought, but I don't think we…' She fought back panic.

'Ah, come on! The last big bash we had here was for your mum, and it lifted everyone's spirits. We are all so happy for you and Sharif. It's like a fairy tale, him finding you and you falling in love…' Zane was coming over all weepy, always one for the melodrama.

The more practical Ivanka chimed in. 'Why not? It's just a party to celebrate your engagement – a few drinks, some nice food, a band maybe?

What's so terrifying about it? All your friends around you, the patients who are able and Nadia. It will be fun, not scary at all.'

Carmel was no longer in awe of her Swedish friend, but she did envy her the confidence she exuded. She had a slight trace of her native Stockholm in her accent, but she seemed to have been everywhere. She casually dropped references to her travels into the conversation, and Carmel felt so unworldly around her. Of course a party wouldn't faze Ivanka, but the prospect made Carmel want to lie in a darkened room.

Carmel desperately tried to find a way out. 'I don't think it would be Sharif's thing, honestly –' she protested, but Zane interrupted her.

'He's fine with it. We asked him already because we knew you'd say that. He said he's happy to have it but it's up to you. So if you don't say yes, you'll be letting him down too. And Sharif loves a party.' Zane winked cheekily.

'Ignore him. He's just looking for an occasion to strut about like a pigeon.'

Zane hooted at Ivanka's word confusion. 'It's a peacock that struts, not a pigeon! Don't you have peacocks in Siberia?' He nudged her playfully. The banter between them was relentless.

'How many more times? I am from Sweden,

not Siberia, and, yes, we do have every kind of bird there, but sometimes I get a teeny bit confused with English, OK? At least I am bilingual, not like you only speaking peacock English...' She winked at Carmel.

'It's pigeon... Ahh...I see what you did there. Very clever...for a Russki, I suppose,' he grumbled good-naturedly. 'Anyway, back to the engagement party – it's going to be great. Pleeease, Carmel, pleease?' He was on his knees in the middle of the Aashna restaurant, making a total show of himself – and them. The patients dotted around smiled; they were used to Zane and his antics. He was like a ray of sunshine around the hospice.

'I hate being the centre of attention, guys, really I do, and all those posh doctor friends sniggering at how Sharif fell for an Irish nobody with only one name...' Carmel was failing miserably to quell their enthusiasm.

'What do you mean? Only one name?' Ivanka was curious.

'Oh, you know, they all seem to be Belinda Parker-Willington and Montgomery Clifton-Barrett. I've been to two doctor social things, and the only one I could talk to was the waitress. We'd have to have all of them too, and it would be dreadful...' She willed them to understand.

'No we don't!' Zane said. 'It's your party – you invite who you like. Sharif isn't really like that at all anyway. You know that he has to go to those events sometimes, but he wouldn't choose the Humpty Bumpingsworth-Bladderfuls of this world and you know it.'

They both giggled at Zane; he really was hilarious.

'OK, so are you saying we can do it if we only have Aashna House staff and patients and Nadia?' Ivanka moved in for the kill.

Carmel knew when she was beaten. 'OK, I suppose so. But low-key, and not too expensive. I don't want flash, OK?'

Zane smirked at Ivanka, high-fiving her theatrically.

'Zane, I mean it. Nothing flamboyant or over the top, just a few friends for a get-together, OK? Promise?'

'Promise, promise! It will be just a stale, curled-up fish-paste sandwich and a cup of lukewarm tap water.'

'I mean it, Zane.' She swatted him on the arm with a grin. 'Please, low-key. Right?'

The other two caught each other's eye once

more and grinned conspiratorially. The good-cop/bad-cop routine had obviously worked.

'Low-key is my middle name,' Zane announced with a flourish. Then he bent to whisper in her ear, 'Actually it's Chilton, after my mum's favourite uncle, but never tell anyone that. Nobody ever dated my Uncle Chilton, and I reckon the name was the biggest problem.'

Carmel giggled as he kissed her cheek, then he went to collect his patient for aqua aerobics in the spa pool.

As Carmel walked across the lawn on her way to the recreation room after lunch, she went over all the things she needed to do. Back in the summer, Daf the principal of the local primary school had approached her and wondered if they could help with the school production of *The Wizard of Oz* the coming year. She's been delighted to get involved and since the return to school, the place was frequently swarming with little kids being measured for costumes. The men of the Men's Shed of Aashna were making he sets and the whole place was buzzing with the excitement of it all. Carmel and Sharif were thrilled how involvement in the production was really giving a powerfully positive energy to the place. They'd ended up taking over the entire costuming, and she was giving lessons on needlework to anyone who was interested. She had organised some snacks for the kids the each time they came to rehearse, and they loved visiting. They stayed for ages, talking to the patients and showing them things on the internet while munching crisps and buns. As the big night drew ever closer, things were somewhat chaotic, with sets falling over, zips bursting and the PA system screeching feedback, much to the delight of the children. The entire staff found reasons to stop by at one time or another to enjoy the fun. The Kaivalya, normally serene and elegant, now looked like a glitter and face-paint explosion. The show was due on stage the following evening, and all the kids' parents and families were coming as well as the staff, patients and their families. The life the production had brought to the hospice was palpable. Even those not involved were excited to see how it all came together.

Carmel was kneeling, mouth full of pins, in front of the Cowardly Lion, who had an almost entirely detached tail. Apparently, he'd closed the toilet door on it, and when he'd turned to see what the problem was, he ripped his tail off as well as tore quite a large hole in the costume. The little boy, Noah, was very upset, so Carmel, along with Jill and Winnie, two patients, were doing their best to soothe him while repairing the damage. Similar catastrophes were being handled throughout the room. Daf assured everyone, big and small, that the dress rehearsal was always a total fiasco but that it would be all right on the night. Carmel hoped she was right, but then realised that once the kids had fun, and the patients saw the fruits of their labours on stage, who cared if it wasn't West End standard?

Finally she took a break from the mayhem, realising she'd not eaten all day. She grabbed a sandwich and a cup of tea from the café and took advantage of the calm before the storm and sat on a bench in the garden, eating her lunch and then kicking off her sandals and resting her eyes. She was trying to practice her mindfulness and being present in order to extract the maximum from her day. Sharif was always trying to get the staff to take time for themselves during the working day; he really believed it led to a more productive, positive atmosphere for everyone if stress could be avoided. He was right, and dealing with death and sadness could be very draining, even in these happy, peaceful surroundings, so she did as he asked whenever she could.

Before she arrived at Aashna, she spent most

of the day on Facebook, chatting in groups. She would have loved to meet those online friends in person. She even once considered asking Bill for the money to do a meditation weekend at a gorgeous Buddhist retreat centre in West Cork but baulked at the last minute. He'd have refused anyway, she'd reasoned with herself; he probably thought anything to do with mind, body and spirit was a load of old codswallop.

As the sun streamed down on her face, she was transported back to Ballyshanley, another lifetime ago. She used to try to dismiss Bill and her old life from her thoughts, but one of Deepak Chopra's guided meditations said that it caused stress to try to constantly police thoughts; instead, he advised just to let them flow into the mind and out again.

She smiled at the thought of explaining meditation to Bill. For him, spirituality was strictly Catholic. They went to Mass at 10:30 every Sunday without fail – Bill, Julia and herself – rain, hail or shine. Carmel tried to find meaning in the words the priest would say, but she failed. She had been brought up in that tradition – daily Mass, weekly confession, the sacraments – for most of her adult life, but it was entirely without meaning for her. Probably because there was never a discussion, never a chance to question or explore the faith; it was just presented as a *fait accompli*. There it was, ready to go, just take it on and off you go. Do what you're told and it will all be fine, but if you dare to stray, by word, deed or thought, then it's 'straight down to the hot fella', as Sister Catherine, her junior infant teacher, would say, describing the eternal fires of hell to five-year-olds with what Carmel now realised was inappropriate enthusiasm.

CHAPTER 8

The production was a triumph and the entire hospice buzzed with the after-glow for days. It was wonderful to see the smiles on the faces of the residents, taken out of their illnesses or worries even for a little while. Imminent death had a way of focusing the mind she realised, and for most people it became not about the big things, but appreciating the little joys of life. A bunch of little children singing 'Follow the Yellowbrick Road' could lift the hardest or saddest of hearts.

She'd come to learn a lot about life and death in the time she'd been in Aashna and what struck her was the ways different people responded to the prospect of what, if anything, came next.

There were people there of all faiths and none, and each was respected. She liked to go to the little chapel at the back of the complex, a multi-denominational place with no iconography or artwork of any one faith but there was a peace there that she loved. She wondered if she's ever felt that in the many Catholic churches of her childhood or adult life and she didn't think she did.

Carmel could recite the prayers of the Mass by heart and say the rosary in her sleep, but it didn't touch the core of her. She would look around at people; some were truly connected to the experience, but most were like her, she imagined, going because it was what you did in an Irish town. Since the scandals of child abuse in recent years, the numbers attending were dwindling, but the Mass was still well attended. The new Irish, those who had moved to Ireland in the last decade from Poland, Lithuania, Latvia and Nigeria, were making their mark on the liturgy as well, so churches were being revitalised by the waves of immigration. She'd seen Masses in Dublin and Cork on TV and they looked lively and connected affairs, but Father Linehan with his monotone voice in Ballyshanley was never going to allow anything like that. Back when she lived in Ireland, she would have loved to not trudge up the hill every Sunday morning, to stay at home and meditate or go for a walk and connect with God that way, but Julia would have had a stroke and Bill would probably have had an even more advanced version of the 'I'm really disappointed how my life turned out' face he always wore.

She recalled how she used to be relieved that at least Julia didn't sit with them at Mass; she was in the choir. Her screechy, reed-thin voice was unmistakable. Carmel was convinced she deliberately tried to drown everyone else out. She would hold the note at the end slightly too long, so for a few seconds, she was doing a solo. Julia thought she was a great singer, but honestly – and Carmel tried to steer away from negative thoughts – Julia sounded like a pig stuck in a gate. Even Bill squirmed a little when the whole congregation was treated to her shrill, ear-splitting version of 'Nearer, My God, to Thee' with the rest of the choir doing their best to drown her out. For most of the choir, and indeed the congregation, she was the petrifying Miss Sheehan, principal of the primary school who terrorised their childhoods, so they were powerless against her.

Carmel recalled one time, a young woman,

Lily something, came to join the choir in the church; her husband was the new Guard in the town and she knew no one, so presumably she thought it might be a way of getting to know people. She had a beautiful voice, and everyone commented after Mass. Carmel could see Julia was fuming. The following week, the choir leader suggested that this Lily do the psalm at Mass, to sing it solo. Julia said nothing at the practice, but when she called to Bill's house after choir, Carmel could see the bile rising up, almost choking her as she droned on and on at Bill. A few weeks later, Lily left the choir and her husband was suspended pending investigation. Apparently someone had made an allegation of misconduct of a sexual nature with a minor. Her husband was training a local under-10s football team. Julia never said anything directly, but she did buy football boots and a new Ireland jersey for one of the Donnelly kids, whose father was an alcoholic, and Carmel was almost sure she put young Donnelly up to saying the Guard did something. Of course nothing came of it, but he was moved on and Julia was left cackling and croaking her way through every solo once more.

Outside Mass one Sunday, a new curate, who was filling in while Father Linehan got his hip replaced, suggested to Julia having a children's choir as well as the adult one at Sunday Mass, but she vetoed that immediately.

'Father Creedon' – she said his name like it hurt her to do so – 'with respect, I know the children of this parish and the houses they come out of in a manner that you simply cannot. I can tell you with one hundred percent certainty that there are no children in this parish who possess the musicality or temperament to be successful in a church choir. I have dedicated my life to the education of the children of Ballyshanley, many of whom are no better than they should be, considering where – and more importantly who – they came from, and one of my God-given talents, my singing voice, has been sorely tested, I can assure you, trying to teach them even the most basic melody.'

Carmel remembered the red spots of indignation on her sister-in-law's gaunt face as she seemed almost to grow taller in her righteous indignation. Her terrifying stare, the severe bun that dragged her sparse hair back over her skull and the cold light-blue eyes that bore down on him did not put the young priest off, however.

'Ah, now, Miss Sheehan, you can't surely be telling me that out of two hundred or so youngsters in the school, not one of them can carry a tune? That seems unbelievable to me.' His smile was gentle, but there was steely determination behind the words. Father Linehan was scared stiff of her and so would never have even attempted the conversation.

'That is' – she enunciated each word as if he were hard of hearing – 'precisely what I am saying, so I think the best thing for you to do is practice your Mass – there were several points today when I felt you were less than confident in your delivery – and leave the choir to me.'

She stalked off then, a mortified Bill and Carmel following behind. Anyone else would have at least exchanged a glance with her husband, but though Bill winced at Julia's screeching at Mass, he would never ally with Carmel against her.

She really was something else, Carmel mused. Carmel was so glad to be in Aashna and not back there. The months since she left Ireland had given her some perspective, and each time she told Sharif a story about her ex-sister-in-law, he was incredulous that Julia could be so manipulative and bossy, and even more disbelieving that the Carmel he had come to know just accepted it.

Being told what to do and expected to obey

without question was so deeply ingrained, she never really thought about it. She didn't like Julia, certainly, but the idea of standing up to her was alien. At least it used to be. She had recently been to see a solicitor who had begun the divorce proceedings, but she had yet to hear anything back, either from him or from Bill. Thoughts of a legal confrontation caused her to worry, but she tried to face the anxiety and tell herself that she would deal with it when she had to. And on top of that, it would be with Sharif and now Joe on her side. She and Joe had settled into an easy friendship, and she loved hearing from him now that he was back in Ireland.

Her reverie was interrupted by her phone beeping. A text from Joe. *Hi, C, how's things today? Had a dream about you last night, where you were singing on stage in a pub in Wicklow?! Mad, eh? Going to Jennifer's for dinner tonight, so am going to tell her about you. Is that OK? x*

She had met him for lunch the day after the big chat, and it had been easy and fun. She told him that her head was in a spin and asked if he'd mind them just getting to know each other before making any big decisions. He was happy to do it, and they ended up drinking a bottle of wine and having a really good laugh. He was charming and funny, and she liked him a lot. Since he went back, he'd been texting and she texted back, chatty newsy texts.

Sure, if you like. I'd like to meet her sometime – she sounds lovely. She paused and thought for a second before adding an 'x'.

Sharif gently teased her about it being like a romance, texting and getting to know each other, but in some ways, he was right. She was nervous of what she said in texts even though she talked so easily with him when they were together. She had never put a kiss on a text to Joe before, though, much to Sharif's amusement; her texts to Sharif were littered with emoticons.

The more time went on, the more she felt like Joe was her real father. He certainly behaved as if he were, telling her to be careful walking at night, or telling her to ask Sharif to examine her when she had a cough. She was fine, but it felt so strange, in a nice way, to have someone care so much. One night, he rang and she noticed he sounded breathless.

'Are you OK? You sound a bit wheezy?'

'Ah, yeah, I've a touch of asthma. I've had it all my life. I'll take a puff of the inhaler now in a second, and I'll be grand again.'

She didn't tell him that she had asthma as well.

Sharif said Dolly didn't, so she wondered if she got it from him.

She put her phone back in her pocket and realised she should be getting going. She and Sharif were leaving for the South of France tomorrow for a whole week, and she couldn't wait for the holiday. They'd chosen the accommodation together off the internet, and Carmel nearly had a fit when she realised the price of the villa with private pool, but Sharif insisted.

'Carmel, OK, I see this is a conversation we need to have.' He looked so serious. 'We are going to get married, yes?'

'Yes, I really hope so, unless you come to your senses,' she tried to joke.

'Firstly, please stop about how you are getting such a catch in me and I'm somehow slumming it. That is ridiculous and not true. We love each other, and that's all there is to it. And on that note, we are an equal team. From now on, we share everything, emotionally, practically and financially.'

She was about to interrupt when he held up his hand, pleading for her silence.

'So you should know this. I have worked very hard for almost twenty years to build this place up. I didn't take holidays, and every spare penny was ploughed back in here. But now, and for the past few years, that hasn't been necessary. Therefore, I have a lot of money – I can show you the bank statements if you want to know specifics – so please, let's just spend it. That is what it's for. I didn't over the years, not because I was saving or anything but because I was so busy I never had time. But now I have you, and I can't tell you how happy that makes me. We are equal. We share everything because I can't be in a relationship with someone who thinks they are not equal to me in every way. Is that OK?' He put his head to one side and looked deeply into her eyes. His silver hair was swept back from his forehead, and his liquid, almost-black eyes searched hers. She knew he was being totally honest.

'But I can't just swan in here and take your money. You worked for that, not me.' She was trying to be reasonable.

'Oh my God, woman! Sometimes you're just infuriating! Why can't you just accept it? I've spent years avoiding gold-digging women who pretended to like me just because I am wealthy, and when I do find someone special, she won't even take my money.'

Sharif had given her a credit card and a debit card for his account, but she preferred to use her own money. It drove him crazy, but she would never again be beholden to anyone, even Sharif, if she could help it.

His frustration gave her a fit of giggles, and they ended up laughing until it turned to passionate kissing.

CHAPTER 9

$\mathcal{C}$armel got up from the yoga mat and stretched. It had been a busy morning dealing with a bit of a disaster with a cookery course where the teacher turned out to be a bit too fond of the cooking sherry. It was solved, but not before a slurring chef made some remarks about the government that were less than savoury. Some of the class participants thought it was funny but one or two were offended so she'd spent the morning smoothing feathers. This afternoon she had a mountain of paperwork to get through so she took advantage of her lunchbreak to get some time on her mat in the garden. The old Carmel would have been far too self-conscious to rest with her eyes closed in public or to stretch like a cat before she came here, but at Aashna, it was the sort of thing people did. As she slipped her feet back into her sandals, and rolled her mat up, she spotted Zane in animated chat on his phone on the other side of the garden. She'd have to have someone keep a very close eye on him if he was organising an engagement party while they were away. She just knew he would use their absence to re-create an unholy alliance of *Strictly Come Dancing* meets Cirque du Soleil.

'Hi, Carmel.'

She was interrupted from her thoughts by Oscar, the yoga teacher, walking barefoot across the grass, Birkenstocks in hand.

'I hear congratulations are in order? Delighted for you both.' His smile was warm and genuine, and not for the first time Carmel felt overwhelming gratitude for the life she now lived.

'Yes, I'm still in shock, to be honest, but yes, it seems like we are doing it.' She chuckled, fizzing inside at the thought of marrying Sharif.

'Well, good on you both. You deserve to be happy. I'd better move on – I've a class in the Kaivalya in ten minutes.' He gave her a wave and wandered off.

She longed for his inner peace; he always seemed so serene and chilled out. He was a fascinating man, and she always enjoyed talking to him. Sometimes if she had time, he taught her a few stretches, so she was building up her 'sun salutes' and 'downward dog'. The first time she tried yoga at home, Sharif came home unexpectedly and she jumped up, flustered and embarrassed, but when he joined in for a few minutes, all her worries disappeared. Her reactions to things were still 'pre-Sharif', as she called it, but she was learning. He wasn't Bill, and she was a grown adult who could make her own decisions. She repeated the mantra often in her head, and gradually, in infinitesimally slow steps, she was starting to believe it.

For once, Sharif was home before her and had made a salad and mixed an omelette, which he put in the pan when she arrived. She loved that he could cook and seemed to enjoy it. Coming from a life with such clearly defined gender roles, it was a revelation to meet a man who ironed his own shirts.

They ate and chatted about their upcoming trip. Just as they were clearing up, his phone beeped. She handed it to him and saw a shadow cross his face as he read the text. It wasn't any of the patients; the staff always used his beeper to contact him if he was needed.

'Everything OK?' she asked, trying not to sound nosey.

'Oh…er…yeah, fine.' His smile recovered instantly, but something had bothered him.

'Are you sure?' Carmel was concerned; she thought he'd been a little preoccupied in recent days.

'Yes, it's probably nothing, but you know Mrs Johnson? She's in the early phases of dementia, as well as having stage three adenocarcinoma.' Noting her look of confusion, he added, 'Lung cancer. Well, her son pulled me aside a few days ago, saying he wasn't happy with the care she was getting and that I wasn't giving her the appropriate medical treatment and all of this. I told him that the care plan had been coordinated not just by me, though I led it, but had input from a variety of health professionals and that his mother was getting the best possible treatment for her condition. He let it go then, but I don't know – there's something about him I just don't trust. Mrs Johnson, when she's lucid, doesn't seem happy with him either, and the staff in the restaurant were saying he was complaining, claiming he'd found a hair in his food… I don't know, he just seems to be a bit of a troublemaker. I've known her for years – she ran the launderette where we used to send the sheets and towels before we built the onsite one. But he's new to me. I don't think I ever even heard her talk about her son, but he's turned up out of the blue and seems to be determined to cause trouble. Marlena just texted me to say he'd been up to reception to say his mother's room was freezing cold and that she was shivering in the bed. That just couldn't be, but she sent someone from maintenance to check it out. The whole building is on a thermostat, and everywhere is fine. I don't know why he's so determined to find fault.'

Carmel felt a surge of protectiveness for Sharif but also for Aashna House. 'God, he sounds awful. I think I know him – kind of rough looking?'

Sharif nodded.

'And his mum is lovely,' Carmel pointed out, 'a really gentle person. Maybe he resents her money being used to pay for her treatment. He sounds like the kind of person who'd be happy to dump her in a state nursing home and let the taxpayer pick up the bill.'

'Well, she was a cleaner here in the hospice when I first started up. Then she took over the launderette up on the high street. She was such a help to me in the early days when I didn't have too many staff. She'd not just clean but she'd feed patients, or push them around the garden in their wheelchairs. She was invaluable and always used to say how lovely it would be to end her days someplace like here. When she got the diagnosis – she was a chain smoker, so it wasn't a surprise really – she came to me and asked if she could come here. Of course I said she could, and so she moved in. Not a mention of this Derek. I know her husband died when she was a young woman, long before I met her. So this guy just shows up. He lives in Hammersmith someplace. And suddenly he's the caring son? She's been here over a year at this stage, and he's only turned up in the last few weeks. I'm not convinced.'

'Well, you know what they say – where there's a will, there's relatives.'

'That's true. I've seen plenty of greed here over the years. But this guy, I don't know, there's something dangerous about him. Also, she doesn't have a bean, so I just can't figure out what he's after. I like his mother a lot, though, and she said she wanted to be treated here, and so treat her we will. I just wish he wasn't part of the equation.' Sharif was normally so unflappable, it was unusual to see him so perturbed.

'I know, but we don't get to pick who comes

through the doors, nor do we get to choose their relatives, unfortunately. I know you're worried, but the others are well able to handle anyone with a problem. Dr Alexander will be here, as well as the junior team, and Nadia is going to move in here for the week just to be extra safe. So let's just enjoy our holiday and try not to think about this place. Johnson has no grounds for complaint – it's not like we're doing anything wrong. His mother, like everyone else here, gets the very best of care, and the staff are aware of him now, so try to put him out of your mind, OK? Your mum told me the last holiday you took was actually to go to a medical conference in Madrid eleven years ago! And, well, I've never had a holiday in my life, so let's just go and relax and have some fun together.'

'Fun? What sort of fun did you have in mind?' He grinned, drawing her close to him.

'Oh, you know, Monopoly, Scrabble, that sort of thing...' She winked, and he lowered his head to kiss her.

* * *

THE HOLIDAY WAS WONDERFUL. They wandered hand in hand around the old city of Saint-Émilion, popping in and out of little caves selling local wines, cheeses and foie gras. Carmel loved it all, though she drew the line at the foie gras once she learned how it was made. They marvelled at the vast cathedral carved out of rock rather than built from the ground up, and they bought baguettes and had picnics on the secluded lawn of their villa. Sharif taught Carmel how to swim in the pool, her first time ever being in water other than a bath. He stopped asking her how it was that she had never been to a beach or a swimming pool or even a cinema because he hated to see the look of shame in her eyes. She tried not to be too wide-eyed and astounded at everything, but it was so hard. She'd never imagined the world was actually like this, so beautiful and warm and welcoming. She realised, living as she had through Facebook during all the years of her marriage, that her world view was kind of distorted. She imagined all conversations to be political in nature, and people to be much more aggressive than they actually were.

She and Sharif sat outside cafés, the sun brightening everything it touched, delighting at the simple beauty of it all. Each day for lunch they'd investigate the mystery of the *plat du jour*. She deliberately never asked what it was and was determined to try as many things as she could. She ended up trying escargot, deliciously swimming in parsley butter; moules served in a large silver bucket and cooked in shallots and white wine, mopped up with crusty baguettes; *confit de canard* that just fell off the bone and melted in the mouth; and the most delicious chips she'd ever tasted. She was sure she must have gained ten pounds and marvelled at the slim French women. How did they live there and stay so slender, she wondered, as she and Sharif tucked into the buttery croissants and *pain au raisin* for breakfast each morning. The little kids blathering away in French fascinated her; she expected the adults to speak the magically romantic language, but the children just blew her away.

CHAPTER 10

*C*armel and Sharif never tired of each other's company. They told stories of their respective childhoods and lives up to the time they met. They talked about Dolly, Nadia, Joe and the whole situation, and Carmel never felt as if she were boring Sharif or droning on. To her utter amazement, he found her a constant source of delight and would often laugh out loud at something she said or stop her mid-sentence to kiss her. She'd never imagined happiness like this existed.

'So...the wedding. What do you want to do?' He was pouring her a glass of Sancerre on the terrace of the villa after they'd strolled back, having had yet another delicious dinner.

'What do you mean, what do I want? To get married as soon as I can…though I'll have to go on a diet at this rate or I won't get a dress to fit me after all this food.' She patted her still-flat belly.

'You have a delicious figure, and anyway, I don't care about that. Those emaciated models never did anything for me. Give me a real woman any day with curves. I've never understood those androgynous females, skin and bone, and I've never met a man who finds them attractive. No, I meant do you want to get married in the UK or Ireland or abroad or where?'

She thought fleetingly of the sad little ceremony seventeen years earlier in the church down the road from Trinity House where she married Bill. 'Not Ireland, anyway, that's for sure. I don't know… What would you like?'

Sharif thought for a moment. 'Well, weddings are generally a bride's domain, especially in my culture, so I haven't thought much about it. But I think I'd like something small, maybe at Aashna? And if it was nice weather, maybe the reception in the grounds. We could have a marquee for the food or something, and set up a bar and a dance floor and all of that. Is that something you'd like? Or would you prefer something else?

'That sounds gorgeous. But there is the business of the divorce first. I know in Ireland it takes years, like you have to be separated for four of the previous five years – I checked it out online.'

'But in the UK, it's nothing like that. You just apply and the court grants it, simple as that. In terms of the marriage being an Irish one, well, that doesn't matter as far as I understand it. You can divorce Bill from there, then get married there because under British law you are divorced.'

'It's so strange I haven't heard from him. I mean, he must have got the letter the solicitor sent by now – it was posted six weeks ago. Because of that, he'll know where I am as he had to put the address on the letter, and I've not heard anything. I know he didn't care for me, but he'd surely want to speak to me. Or even Julia would. Don't get me wrong – I'd dread to get a letter from either of them. But even so, it's weird, don't you think?'

Sharif sighed and sat down opposite her, giving her the glass of wine and taking her other hand. 'To be honest, I find the entire relationship weird. The idea that a red-blooded man would have you beside him in bed every night for seventeen years and never laid a finger on you – I just don't get it. We're simple creatures, carnal, and either his restraint is remarkable or there is something deeply wrong with him. I suspect the latter. And as for that witchy sister of his, I mean, what on earth is that all about? She was horrible to you because she wanted to be some kind of pseudo wife to her own brother? As I said, the entire thing is a mystery to me.'

Carmel smiled. Sharif had had a few glasses of wine with dinner, so he was a little more candid than normal. Generally, he just remained silent on the subject of Bill and her years with him. 'I just hope he agrees and lets the divorce go through. Every time there was a referendum in Ireland on the subject, and there were three, it was the Church that came out most strongly against it. It was only finally allowed in 1995, but the rules are still fairly draconian. Bill and Julia are pillars of the community and of the Church, and even though people in Ireland have been getting divorced for over a decade now, in certain sections of society, there is still a stigma. Bill and Julia would be part of those sections.'

'So better to stay miserable than be free to find happiness elsewhere? Seems mad to me.'

'More or less, yes. What God has joined together and all of that.'

Carmel took a sip of her wine; it was delicious. The scent of the lavender that ringed the garden was released by the evening sun, and Sharif was captured in a beautiful buttery light. 'You look like an angel,' she said as she held up her hand to shield her eyes from the setting sun. 'Maybe you are, a gorgeous, sexy angel sent to me by my mother. Sometimes I really think that. Like, I know I never met her, but in Aashna and when I'm with you and Nadia and even Joe, I feel her and sense that she's with me. Do you believe in all of that?'

Sharif thought for a moment. 'I do, I suppose. I was reared a cultural Muslim, though not a very devout one, but like you with Catholicism, I have more or less walked away from it. The faith itself is not the problem – in fact, it has some good advice about how to live, just as the Bible does – but I want no part of what it means in the modern world. Religion only divides people in my view. And something I have observed in all my years in oncology and palliative care is that no matter who we are, men or women, Black or White, old, young, rich, poor, Christian, Hindu, Muslim, atheist, whatever, we all are born the same way and we all die the same way. We all want to be happy, to be loved, for our families and friends to be safe and well. Our bodies may look different on the outside, but we all have the same internal organs – inside we are all the same.

'As for the idea of angels and spirits and all of that, absolutely. If you have seen as many people die as I have, you couldn't think otherwise. Something often happens in the last moments, a peacefulness, a joy. The pain just seems to go, and the person is at peace. They are moving on. To where or what, I don't know, but this is not the end. You saw it with Brian, but I've seen that same thing, many, many times, with people from all sorts of backgrounds.' He closed his eyes, enjoying the warm night breeze.

'Do you think Dolly sent you to me?' Carmel asked quietly.

'I don't honestly know. What I do know is she wanted so desperately to find you. And I know that she loved me. It does seem strange that in all the times she went over there and searched, she got nowhere and then that I found you in a Facebook group. I'm not even on Facebook – there's an Aashna page but someone else manages it. But I do believe the dead are not gone, that their energy, the essence of a person, continues on in some form. But whether they can influence things in this world is the great unknown.

'So to answer your question, I couldn't be

sure. I am first and foremost a clinician. I believe strongly in science, in evidence. So I'd probably be drummed out of the Medical Council for saying so, but possibly she did, yes.' He topped up her glass and continued. 'Now on that note, Joe and the DNA test. Obviously, it's your decision, but have you come to any conclusions about what you want to do?'

Carmel sighed. She had thought so much about it but was no closer to a resolution. 'I don't know, Sharif. Honestly, I have no idea what's for the best. He is wonderful, and I feel a real connection to him. You know he told me the other day on the phone that he has asthma? Immediately, I was happy, not that he has it, but that I might have got it from him, as you said Dolly didn't have it. But then maybe his father had it and that's where it comes from. I don't know, Sharif. It's all such a muddle. I want him to be my dad, but if he's not, then all of that is fake, isn't it? I don't mean he's a fake, but I mean, what's the point? I'm forty years old, I don't need a dad now, so it's not like he can be a surrogate father. Like, it would be different if I were a kid. Am I making sense?'

'Yes and no. I understand that you want him to be your father and you feel like if he is, then you could build up a loving relationship with him, so you are afraid to do the test in case of the alternative and it is his father who is your biological father. But have you thought of this? I'm not advocating any position, just a thought, but Joe feels like he is your father. He's told you so. And you feel that he is, or maybe you wish it to be the case. So why not leave it at that? What good would finding out do?' He leaned over and took her hand. 'I know people always say truth is the best way forward, people should know the truth and so on, but I'm not too sure about that. I'll tell you something that nobody knows. When my parents were young and I was just a child, my father had an affair. He told me when he was dying – he needed to confess to someone, I think. And when I asked him if my mother ever knew, he said he didn't tell her because it would only have hurt her. He loved her deeply, always did, but he was foolishly flattered by another woman's attentions and so was unfaithful. It was over in a matter of weeks and it meant nothing to him. He explained to me that his punishment was to bear the burden of the guilt on his own, to spare my mother the pain of his betrayal. Of course I was furious at first and accused him of not telling the truth to protect himself, not me or my mother, and I stormed out. But then I spoke to Dolly. She was like the grave if you confided in her – you could guarantee her silence.

'She said to me, "Sharif, the truth is overrated. It usually hurts, and more often than not does no bloody good at all. Sometimes the best way to love someone is to protect them from the truth. Your father is very sorry for the mistake he made. He regrets it and he never did it again. Your mother loves him and you and the life you've all had together all these years. Breaking that up over something so inconsequential as a brief affair with someone he didn't love would be to make you and Nadia pay for a crime you didn't commit. He did wrong – he knows that and he's full of regret – but he's a human being and humans make mistakes. He chose to bear the guilt himself and spare both of you. You should be thanking him, not angry at him."

'And after a while, I calmed down and realised she was right. It would have broken our family. My mother is a proud woman and could never have taken him back, and then what would her life, and my life, have been like? My father worked so hard for me to go to university, and every penny he earned was for us. He never bought things for himself – he had the same car for fifteen years – but he would spare no expense when it came to my mother or me. He was a good man.'

Carmel heard the catch in Sharif's voice and knew how private he was, so the fact that he confided something like that in her made her feel so loved and trusted. 'He did the right thing,' she said. 'Your mum talks so fondly of him, and it's clear she adored him.'

'She did. We all did. Dolly too. He was so good to us all, and he carried that guilt at his one transgression his whole life. That whole experience has made me rethink the value of the truth.'

Carmel got up and went to sit on his lap, then put her arms around him as he rested his head on her breast. Together, they sat in the silence of a fragrant French evening.

CHAPTER 11

*T*he holiday really refreshed them both and brought them even closer. Sharif talked about Jamilla, and about how losing her was the worst thing that had ever happened to him. Carmel just listened, and even though she knew Sharif had once loved Jamilla so much, she didn't feel the confusion and hurt she felt about Bill and Gretta, probably because Sharif was so anxious to point out that she was dead and they were living. They owed it to her, and to Dolly, to live the best life they could.

Two days after they returned, they were having breakfast before work.

'I was thinking of inviting Joe and maybe his

kids over for the engagement party. What do you think?'

'Sure, good idea. He's told them about you, so I'm sure they're curious. I know I would be.' Sharif was talking to her but reading something on his phone at the same time.

'Yes, well, he said they were OK about it but...' She stopped. 'Sharif, what's the matter? You seem worried.'

'Oh, I asked Marlena to keep a log of all the complaints coming in from this Derek Johnson, and she's just emailed it to me. He claims that his mother wasn't given her medicine at the right time, the room is too cold, the food is making her sicker, staff are rude, the physio is too rough, and he said he didn't want Ivanka working with her any more, something about her swearing at his mother! He mentioned something to her about malpractice – he actually used that word. This is outrageous. I can't have this any longer. I'm going to speak to him today. If he is not happy with the service we provide, then maybe he... Oh, I don't know... Mrs Johnson wants to be here, and she expressly asked me. But he's her next of kin, and now her dementia is advancing and there doesn't appear to be any other family. This is such a mess.

I just have a feeling he's building up to something.'

'Like what? I mean, he can't do anything to hurt you, can he?'

'Well, a malpractice suit is every physician's worst nightmare. It's damaging beyond repair, even if it's totally groundless. It can drag on and on in court, and the patients' advocacy groups are very resourceful if they take up someone's cause. Even a complete lie could close us down.'

She'd never seen him so solemn. Surely that couldn't be true? Sharif was a wonderful doctor and Aashna House was such a special place; surely one malicious person couldn't tear down all he'd built just out of spite. 'But why would he want to, even if it was possible?' Carmel couldn't understand such viciousness.

'Well, the deal is that if people want to come here, the state funds it partially, but in return, their pension and whatever income they might have is taken into consideration. The state looks at people's financial situation, and then based on what they can contribute, they make up only the difference. If he had his way, he'd probably take her home and say he'd care for her, which he wouldn't be able to do even if he wanted to, but he would then inherit the house and whatever bit of money she has. You'd be amazed at how many children of elderly sick parents are against them coming here, not because the offspring themselves have to pay, but because they see it as eating into their inheritance.'

'Oh, what a nasty piece of work. How could he do that to his own mother?'

'Easily. He sees her death as a windfall for him, and he wants to make sure he gets the maximum amount possible. By complaining that everything is wrong here, that I'm being negligent or unprofessional or whatever, he has grounds to remove her from our care. Poor Mrs Johnson is not lucid most of the time now, so she's easily manipulated. That's a very sad element of this, but worse, there's the threat of him reporting me as an incompetent physician, and that would be a disaster.'

'Don't you have insurance against that? And as you say, Mrs Johnson's needs are complex and there's no way he'd be able to take care of her properly.'

'Yes, but the problem is the process takes so long and people believe in the "no smoke without fire" theory. Even if the accusation is totally false, the damage done to reputation is irreparable. Even one malpractice case has been known to close down so many healthcare professionals. As for him taking care of her, well, I dread to think. She would be in terrible pain if it's not managed, and she's not lucid most of the time so wouldn't even be able to complain or get help.'

Carmel tried to think. It was an area about which she knew nothing, but she desperately wanted to help Sharif. 'Perhaps you talking to him isn't the best idea. You know, it might end up being used against you, especially if you get cross or whatever. Why don't I have a go, you know, casually. I could be popping into Mrs Johnson, and I'll try to strike up a conversation, see if I can't get some information out of him? I promise I won't make the situation worse. If I can't get him to open up, then fine, we try another way, but it might be worth a shot? It could be that he's just an old loudmouth, looking for something to moan about, but he won't go any further.'

Sharif thought for a moment. 'Maybe you're right – I hope you are. But just be careful. He's very aggressive, and if this does go to court afterwards and it emerges, as it's bound to, that you and I are in a relationship, then it could be misconstrued. In the meantime, I'm going to call my solicitor to get his take on it, see if there isn't something to be done before this Derek Johnson does anything worse.'

Carmel hated to see Sharif threatened in this way. He was such a good man, and such a conscientious doctor; the idea that someone could just come along and tell a bunch of lies and threaten everything he worked so hard to create seemed so very unfair.

She made it her business to pop into Mrs Johnson several times during the day, but of her son there was no sign. The day flew by, just like all the others.

Eventually, she spotted Derek Johnson leaving the hospice and getting into a very old car. Carmel approached him as he was throwing an Aashna House plastic bag, which probably contained Mrs Johnson's clothes for washing, into the back. Carmel noticed several other bags like it littering the back seat. There was a laundry service, but in general, patients' families were encouraged to do the patient's laundry at home, and most people did. Clearly, this Johnson was taking the dirty clothes but not doing much with them. The entire floor of the car was covered in junk-food wrappers and beer cans.

'Hi, Mr Johnson. I'm Carmel. I work here. I was wondering how your mum was today?'

He looked warily at her. 'What's it to you? You're not a nurse or a doctor.'

Carmel tried to ignore the rudeness in his tone and the dismissive attitude. Not only was he an odious personality, but he was a physically repulsive specimen as well. His grubby Guns N' Roses T-shirt didn't quite cover his voluminous beer belly, and his trousers were shiny with wear and, she suspected, dirt. He badly needed a haircut, greasy curls almost reaching his shoulders, and he was unshaven. He smelled fairly pungent as well. But Carmel was determined to be pleasant and to keep the conversation light. 'No, no, I'm not, but I organise the events here.' She nailed a smile on her face.

'Look, my mother ain't goin' to be goin' to any events. She's nearly dead, thanks to this excuse for a hospital.'

'Well, perhaps if you and I had a chat, maybe we could address some of the issues you appear to be having?' Carmel knew she was grasping at straws, but she was trying to get something she could take back to Sharif.

'You're having a laugh, right? I ain't got nuffin to say to you or to that Paki what owns this place. Why don't you lot all bugger off back where you came from, eh?' He slammed the door and drove away, the car backfiring and emitting bilious black smoke.

Carmel stood in the car park, stunned.

'Carmel! You OK?' Zane called as he ran across the car park. 'I saw him talking to you. Was he having a go?'

Carmel relayed the conversation, incredulous that someone could be that horrible.

'Oh, welcome to my world, darlin'. It happens. Most people are nice, glad to live in a multicultural society and all of that, but there's always a few, and he's one. Don't give him the time of day. He's horrible to everyone – it's not personal.' He grinned and gave her a peck on the cheek. 'He called me the N-word the other day.'

'He didn't!' Carmel was shocked.

'Water off a duck's back. Have you seen the state of him? And the smell off of him? He's mingin'. I don't rent out space in my head to people like him. I got enough problems. Now, it's knocking-off time. A post-work drink to settle our nerves after all of this?' He winked at her and flashed her one of his irresistible grins.

CHAPTER 12

*C*armel had been going to find Sharif to tell him of the exchange, but she decided to leave it. She hadn't found anything out apart from the fact that Johnson was a racist, ignorant pig. Anyway, Sharif was upstairs at a multidisciplinary conference with the team to discuss some patients with very complex needs, so he wouldn't be home for another two hours at least. She might as well go and try to forget about Johnson. 'Sure. Will we text Ivanka?'

'She and Ivy are already there – it's been one of those days.' He threw his eyes heavenward dramatically and linked her arm as they walked to the pub.

'Congratulations on your promotion. Sharif told me,' Carmel said.

'Thanks. I never would have got through the exams without Ivanka, though – don't tell her that obviously. But whenever I wanted to go out, she made me stay in and study.'

Zane had been studying nursing at night for the past four years and had recently graduated. Once he qualified, Sharif immediately promoted him from care assistant to the nursing staff.

'Do you want to come to my conferring?' he asked casually.

'Me?' Carmel was surprised. 'But shouldn't your family be there?'

'Yeah, usually, but I'm not going to say anything to my mum. She'd feel like she should go, and my old man would make life hard for her – best she doesn't know. So I was going to invite you and Ivanka instead. I've told her I'm gonna tell people you're my mum and she's my nana.' He laughed.

'Oi, cheeky!' She nudged him in the ribs.

'Ow, that hurt, and you might have damaged my costal cartilages.'

'Oh, that's how it's going to be, is it, now that you're medically qualified?' Carmel demanded.

'Don't you raise your larynx-originated orations at me,' he quipped.

'Oh no,' Carmel groaned. 'It's going to be a long night, I can tell.'

'Will you come then?' he asked, and she saw that trace of vulnerability that so endeared him to everyone.

'I would love to, but…' she began.

'But what?'

'Well, I just think…' She paused, wondering if she should go on. 'Your mum loves you, right?'

He nodded.

'And I know your dad is difficult and all of that, but don't you think your mother would like to see her son graduate? Doesn't she deserve to sit there and feel proud of you?'

'But my dad…'

'Is a different person with his own thing going on, but your mum has stood by you. She's accepted you and loved you for who you are. I think she'd like to put on a nice dress and clap when her boy goes up to get his parchment. I never knew my mum and I doubt I'll ever know what it feels like to see your child achieve something, but I know this much. If I had a kid, no matter what the achievement was, I'd be there. So I think at least give her the chance.'

Tears shone in Zane's dark eyes. He couldn't speak but he nodded, and she knew she had been right to say it.

* * *

THE DAYS FLEW BY. The school production had built a bond between the school and the hospice so visits from the children had become a regular thing. Even those who were too ill to participate were enjoying the buzz created by the kids around the clinic. Daf was so grateful for their help with the musical she had the children make a huge poster, full of drawings and messages for everyone at Aashna; it proudly took up most of one wall of the Kaivalya. Several of the older residents had been hesitant at first to get involved with the children, but the little ones broke down barriers effortlessly, and Carmel was so gratified when even the most reticent or grumpy of patients asked her when the children were coming. The restaurant made chicken nuggets and chips as well as pizza, on the days Daf brought them to visit and the staff found – to the chef's astonishment – that everyone seemed to opt for the kid food on those days. At Carmel's suggestion, they'd even invested in a wood-fired pizza oven, so pizza night was Thursdays; people could make their own from a variety of toppings.

Carmel had a few things to organise for the next week's French course, so she needed the calm of her office. Roger, the chef, was French and his cuisine was legendary, so he was giving five half-hour cookery demonstrations. The patients were looking forward to it, though it was unlikely any of them would be using their new skills again. Roger was a quintessentially French character, with a pencil-thin moustache and an air of ennui, but it was an act and he made everyone laugh.

As Carmel walked to her office, she tried to mentally work out the schedule of French language conversation classes, a talk on wine and the cookery classes. She tried to focus but the Derek Johnson situation was never far from her mind. There was nothing she could do about that, so she just tried everything she could to remove any other responsibilities from Sharif's shoulders.

Oscar waved as she passed the sun-filled yoga studio. It was one of her favourite rooms, with bleached pine floorboards, polished and varnished to a shine, and one full wall of glass that overlooked the gardens. There were comfortable chairs around the walls and a beautiful grand piano in one corner, but the main floor area was clear. There were all sorts of activities that took place in there, from meditation to tai chi, ballroom dancing to yoga.

'Hi, Oscar, how's it going?' She popped her head round the door.

'Hi, Carmel. All good, thanks. How about you?' Oscar had a way of asking how one was that made her feel like he really wanted to know.

'Fine.' Sharif had spoken to a few of the staff about the situation with Johnson, but she wasn't sure who. She suspected he'd probably told Oscar, but she didn't want to say anything just in case. 'I hope you're going to make the engagement party on Friday? Zane, Ivanka and now Ivy have taken over the organisation, so I'm in the horrors about what they've planned. They are so enthusiastic, and I need someone calm by my side.'

'I certainly am, wouldn't miss it. I'll have to go home after the strippers, though...' He laughed out loud at the look of dismay on Carmel's face. 'Oh, I fear I've said too much.'

'Tell me you're joking! Honestly, with Zane, anything is possible.'

The closer the party got, the more stressed she became. Joe was coming with his two kids, and that terrified her. He'd said that they were fine about everything, but she didn't know what he'd told them. She had tried to pluck up the courage to ring him but hesitated and stopped each time she was halfway through punching in the number. She knew she was being stupid. Texting she could handle, but conversations, either on the phone or in person, about stuff she hadn't even processed herself yet, were just too much. Then there was the thought of being the centre of attention; Zane even said she'd have to make a speech, which actually made her feel nauseous. Sharif knew how she felt and offered to call it all off, but she said she'd feel even more ridiculous, and anyway, everyone was looking forward to it. Everyone except her.

Oscar, realising she was upset, led her to a sofa at one end of the studio and sat her down. 'Hey, are you OK? You look a bit stressed. Don't worry, Carmel, it's just a party, a bunch of people who like you and Sharif very much and are happy to see how much you mean to each other. It's going to be fun. Ignore Zane. He's just winding you up – you know what he's like. There are no strippers or speeches or anything, I promise you.

Sharif has spoken to them and said it's to be kept low-key and not too many people. Ivy and Ivanka will curb the heights of Zane's enthusiasm, and even if they don't, the rest of us will. OK?'

Carmel shut her eyes and took a deep breath. She needed to centre herself, to find her inner calm. 'OK.' She gave Oscar a watery smile. 'I know he means well, and he's been such a great friend to me since I got here – you all have. I never had a bunch of friends before. That sounds mad, I know, but where I grew up, it wasn't encouraged, and then afterwards, well, it was a kind of empty life. So I'm just not used to this, and I'm a bit socially pathetic, to be honest.'

Oscar walked over to the grand piano, took a mirror off of it, and walked back to her, handing it to her. 'Look.' His voice was gentle.

'At what?' Carmel was confused.

'Look and tell me what you see.'

'Myself. I see my face.'

'Who are you, Carmel?' he asked in his soft Scottish burr, rolling his Rs.

She looked up into his kind face as the silence hung between them. 'I have no idea,' she whispered softly.

'Well, isn't it about time that you found out? What the world sees is a kind, funny, beautiful woman, who has come here, to this place, the place that the mother you never knew loved, to be with a very special man. We all like you, Carmel, and nobody thinks of you the way you seem to think of yourself. My wish for you is to see that, to see when you look in the mirror what the rest of us see, what Sharif sees. Anyone who cares for him knows how he has dedicated his entire life to this place. It's not just a hospice – you've seen it with your own eyes. It's something much more enriching and fulfilling than just some place people go to die. People find their life's purpose here, often at the very closing of their lives, and they die with dignity and peace. Sharif created that. He doesn't care a jot for wealth or flashiness – you know that about him. He could be a multimillionaire, but he allows so many people in here free of charge and never mentions it. Sharif sees goodness, kindness, fun, humility, humanity in you, Carmel, and so do we. Nobody here judges you because of your background. The only one doing that is you.'

Such kindness and friendship should have made her feel better but didn't. What on earth was wrong with her? She had a life now, one she could never have dreamed of, and here she was being a big baby over everything. She was so angry with herself that she berated herself and wished she could be the woman Sharif deserved. Tears came unbidden. 'I'm sorry, Oscar.' She wiped her eyes roughly. 'I'm just being stupid. Ignore me.'

'You're not being stupid,' he insisted gently. 'You're just feeling a wee bit worried about a big event coming up and you're talking it out with a friend. We all need that, Carmel, me, Sharif, Zane, everyone. Nobody is as composed as what we present to the world, and what happens to us in childhood matters.'

'Maybe you're right. It's just there's a lot going on at the moment.'

'Isn't there always? Anyway, if you ever want to talk, you know where I am.'

'Thanks. I really mean it. Thank you.' She looked at his kind face and wondered aloud, 'Have you got kids, Oscar?'

He grinned. 'Yes, three. Two girls from my first marriage, Ellie and Daniella, and while I was a total nightmare, my ex was a trooper. Not only that, she never turned them against me, which she could so easily have done. I would have deserved it. But I have a great relationship with them. They stay with me at weekends, and we try to co-parent as much as possible. They're thirteen and eleven now, so they can be challenging, but they are great and I adore them. And I also have a two-year-old son with my partner, Caroline. He's called Teddy and he's fabulous. How about you?'

'Me? No. My ex had two daughters, twins actually, but they really missed their mother so they never took to me, I'm afraid. They have an aunt they're close to, so I wasn't needed. Your kids are so lucky, having you as a dad. I bet they'll grow up really happy, confident people.'

Oscar smiled, and Carmel liked how it crinkled the skin at the sides of his eyes.

'I hope so,' he said. 'We're all doing our best to lay the foundations of that anyway. It's so important to build kids up in childhood. Otherwise, life can be very hard. My mum was accused once of giving me and my brothers a superiority complex, and she explained that there was a very hard world out there only too willing to knock the confidence out of anyone, and so if the sense of self-worth wasn't built up at home, then what did you have to fight with? Of course, I grew up to be a total plonker, obsessing about money and deals and thinking I was so important, so maybe it backfired a bit, but I'm reconciled to that now. It took time, though, Carmel, and a lot of self-examination to get to here. I don't know your background, apart from the bit you've told me about growing up in care and an unhappy marriage, but it sounds to me like you need some investment in yourself. See someone, talk to them, work this stuff out for yourself. We all deserve to be happy, Carmel, but it's something generated inside – the outside world can't provide it. Money, success, power, even other people can't make us truly happy. We need to find that in here.' He pointed at his chest, and Carmel knew he was right.

'Thanks, Oscar.' She stood up, and he drew her into a hug. Normally, physical contact like this with anyone except Sharif made her squirm – she never knew what she should do in return – but this time she just relaxed. She'd been hugged more in the six months she'd been at Aashna than in the forty-one years before that. 'I never got a hug as a kid. Or as an adult, now that I think of it.' The words were out before she even realised it.

Oscar sighed but didn't let her go. 'The wonderful thing about this life we've been given, Carmel, is we can change it. We can reinvent ourselves as often as we want to. It's not easy – we need to let go of a lot of nonsense that hurt us in the past – but it can be done. If I can go from an arrogant city broker, obsessed with power and status and things, to the man I am today, then you can be a happy fulfilled woman who believes she is worthy of someone's love. Regret and guilt are two of the most pointless emotions. The past is over. It happened, and nothing we can do will change it, but we can decide to not let it be our future. It's a long road ahead, but you can do it.'

CHAPTER 13

he moment was interrupted by Carmel's phone ringing. It was Marlena on reception.

'Hi, Marlena.'

'Carmel, I'm so sorry about this, but someone is here demanding to see you. I told her you'd call her if she left a number, but she's most insistent. Can you come up?' Marlena, usually unflappable, sounded harassed.

'Sure. I'm on the way.' Carmel turned to Oscar. 'Thanks for the advice, Oscar – I'll do it. I better go. Someone is looking for me. Marlena sounded a bit stressed. Some of these salespeople can be very pushy.'

'See you, Carmel. Nice to chat.'

She hurried across the grounds towards the large glass reception area. It was beautiful inside, with tropical plants thriving in all the heat and sunshine captured by the glass-domed roof. She'd become accustomed to sales reps coming and trying to sell various products to Aashna House, and she surprised herself at how forceful she could be in return when people were too pushy. She went in the back and stopped dead in her tracks.

'Carmel. So this is where you've been hiding.' Julia's words dripped icy disdain as she stood squarely in front of her.

'Julia... How... I wasn't expecting...' Carmel could hear the tremor in her voice.

Her sister-in-law looked at her as if she were a very slow five-year-old. 'You sent a letter, or at least some solicitor did? Or do you not recall the tiny matter of your husband and family in Ireland? Did you just expect us to pay up and walk away?'

Visitors and various staff members were milling around, and Carmel really didn't want to have this conversation here, in public. 'Em, right... Can we go to my apartment – it's not far – to talk...' She was sweating and could feel the rivulets of perspiration running down her back.

'Yes. Let's go to *your apartment*, Carmel.' Julia's tone and heavy emphasis suggested the idea of Carmel having an apartment was highly suspect.

Carmel didn't dare catch Marlena's eye as she quickly exited reception. Not a word passed between her and Julia as they walked towards the residences. Panic rose inside her.

Julia looked even more angular and pointy today. She was in her best coat, a black velvet thing that made her look like an angry crow, and on her head she wore a ridiculous hat. What on earth was she doing here? What did she want? Was she going to try to take her back to Bill?

Don't be stupid, she told herself as she almost sprinted to her apartment. *She can't make you do anything. She can't force you to go back. You're a grown woman with your own right to live wherever you want...* Although she told herself that often, she wished she could believe it.

It took three goes to get the key in the lock, but eventually she managed it. Carmel opened the door, and Julia walked past her into the lounge. Carmel caught the look of surprise in Julia's eyes at the beauty of her home. The oatmeal sofas, the flat-screen TV, the lovely rosewood dining table and the high-gloss fitted kitchen with French doors out to the courtyard were a far cry from the 1970s time warp that was Bill's dreary farmhouse.

'Can...can I get you a drink? Tea?' Carmel knew she was coming across as pathetic but couldn't help herself. She should throw Julia out, not offer her tea.

'No. I don't want anything.' Julia spoke slowly, taking everything in.

Thank goodness Carmel had put the framed photo taken in France of herself and Sharif in the bedroom. A couple they'd struck up a conversation with offered to take it, and it was a really nice one. Nadia had got it framed for them as an engagement gift. Carmel felt a knot of anxiety rise up like bile within her as Julia's eyes rested on the 'Congratulations! You're Engaged' cards on the shelves beside the TV.

'So whose hospitality are you encroaching on now? This is clearly not your apartment, whatever you may want me to believe, and I doubt that any couple, recently engaged, wants you hanging around.'

Carmel knew she should say something, something to defend herself from Julia's scathing remarks, but she just couldn't. She busied herself with cups, despite the rude rebuff of her offer of a drink. Hands shaking, she dropped a mug from the countertop, where it smashed on the floor.

Julia's look said it all: *Typical Carmel, can't do anything right.*

'So are you going to explain yourself? What are you trying to do over here in this godforsaken place?'

If anywhere was godforsaken, Carmel wanted to yell, it was the miserable farmhouse on a lonely bit of a farm in Ballyshanley, County Offaly. Aashna was beautiful; even Julia could see that. And for some reason, the insults about Aashna were more cutting than those directed at her.

Carmel brushed up the shards of mug in silence, her head down, and opened the bin.

'You seem to have your feet firmly under the table here anyway, however you've managed it. It's very sterile, though, no personality. And that's a very stupid colour for a sofa – sure it will be filthy in no time. I'm surprised you haven't spilled something all over it already as you're so clumsy.' The suggestion was clear that Carmel was behaving deceitfully, hoodwinking some innocent with her imagined tale of woe.

After years of living with Gretta's knick-knacks and ornaments, Carmel loved the bare-surfaced simplicity of the apartment. Sharif too was not a collector of things; his clothes, his washing things and a few books were all he owned really. He loved his clothes – she'd found that so funny at the beginning, that he had a style all his own – but whenever he bought something new, which he did often, he donated something else to the charity shop on the high street.

Julia's inquisitive and judgemental gaze stopped to rest on an Islamic painting hanging beside the French doors. Nadia had brought it back from Karachi, from her parents' house when they died. When she gave it to Carmel, she explained that where she had placed it was the Qibla, the place where Muslims would pray in the house. Nadia knew that Sharif wasn't religious, but he and Carmel were delighted to accept the gift. When Nadia asked if Carmel would object to it being up in their living room, Carmel had explained that people often had religious paintings or statues in their houses in Ireland as well, even if they weren't religious at all. Sometimes they were family heirlooms or just a tradition. Sacred Heart pictures, crucifixes and images of the Virgin Mary were common in Irish homes, and so she was happy to have the symbol of Sharif's culture in theirs. Besides, she loved the blue and white geometric design; it was soothing to look at.

'It's from Pakistan,' she managed to say as Julia's eyes rested on the picture.

'Really? It looks like something the children would do in school. Pakistan, you say? And what, might one ask, would you know about Pakistan?'

This was it. She had to summon up the courage to tell Julia the truth. 'Sharif Khan, the doctor who runs this place, is from there.' She was disgusted at herself. Why couldn't she have said, 'Sharif, my fiancée, owns it – his mother gave it to us as a gift'? Because she was feeble, that was why.

'And does this man allow you to live here in return for working in this hospital, or whatever it is?'

'Yes, I am the events manager here.'

'Pah!' Julia barked. 'You are, in your eye, the manager of anything. Listen to me, Carmel Murphy, I know what you are. I've always known what you are. You might have fooled these eejits over here, thinking you're all sweetness and light, but I know your game.'

'I don't know what you're talking about. I don't have a game... I don't want –' Carmel began.

'Oh, don't you now? Is that why you sent a solicitor's letter to my poor brother, demanding half of our family farm? Because you have no plans, is that it? You must think I'm a total simpleton.'

'I did not demand anything. I saw the letter myself. The solicitor was simply asking to start divorce proceedings, and so he wanted a valuation of the land and so on. It's standard practice...' Carmel wished she felt as confident as she sounded. She had been nervous when the solicitor sent the letter, despite him explaining that it was perfectly routine.

'Standard practice! Listen to yourself! Standard practice indeed. That is our family's land – it has been in the Sheehan family for four generations. And you think a nobody like you, born out of dirty carnal sin, is going to take it away from us? Do you?' She crossed to the kitchen and stood four-square before Carmel.

'Look, I just want a divorce. I'm sure Bill does too. I want to get on with my life and let him get on with his. I've no interest in that farm, but, Julia, it's Bill's farm anyway, not yours. We've had this conversation already. Bill and I will come to an arrangement...' Carmel was trying to be reasonable.

'Bill will do no such thing! Not while I have breath in my body. You tried to kill me once – I won't forget that. You're lucky I didn't go to the Guards, but you caused enough drama and I didn't want to add to poor Bill's problems. That land was my mother's – my father only married in. It is as much mine as it is Bill's, and I won't stand by and have our land carved up to pay off a gold-digging tramp.' She grabbed Carmel's arm and squeezed.

'Julia, let me go...' Carmel's arm was really hurting; the woman was surprisingly strong.

'Take your hands off her immediately!' Sharif exclaimed as he burst into the apartment.

Carmel shook Julia off and ran to him, knocking Julia off her feet in the process. The situation would have been funny if Carmel weren't so shaken. Julia fell backwards over the arm of the couch and looked most undignified, legs in the air, as she tried unsuccessfully to right herself. She fumed as her skirt rode up and her thick brown tights and beige corselette were on display.

Sharif made no effort to help her up, instead putting his arms around Carmel and addressing Julia in a voice Carmel had never heard him use before. 'I have no idea who on earth you are, but get off our property this moment or I will call the police and have you arrested for assault.' Carmel had never seen Sharif so angry. Fury glittered in his dark eyes and his voice was cold as steel. He kept his arms around Carmel, protecting her.

'And who do you think you are? You will do nothing of the kind.' Julia struggled to right herself. Eventually, she was upright, but two red spots of fury glowed in her cheeks. She had been humiliated, and Carmel knew this wasn't going to be taken lightly. 'I was speaking to my brother's wife, and if you knew what she had done, then you'd not be so quick to defend her.'

'Oh, so you must be the dreaded Julia. I recognised you from Carmel's description. I am Dr Sharif Khan.' Carmel noted the look of shock on Julia's face that Sharif knew who she was.

'Oh, I'm sure she's made up plenty of lies about me and poor Bill to make you feel sorry for her and give her a job and a flat. She's good at that, taking advantage of people's generosity. She's always going to land on her feet, that one – a bloodsucker is all she is. But it is all just that, total lies, and if she thinks we're going to take this lying down, her sending solicitor's letters and threatening Bill, well then, she has another think coming. I'd say you should check who you have as a lodger or as a cleaner or whatever she is, because little Carmel is not the sweet innocent she's pretending to be, I can tell you that.'

Sharif stared at Julia. 'Carmel, *my fiancée*' – he emphasised the words deliberately and watched the news penetrate Julia's self-righteous indignation – 'told me about you and how you treated her. How you constantly criticised her, how you tried to dictate her every move. How you're so greedy, you're determined to get that scrap of land, and how all this concern for your brother is a joke – you just have your eye on what you'd like to get when he dies. And she told me about Bill, treating her more as a slave than a wife. She has told me everything, and I know she is telling the truth –'

'Oh, well, isn't that the right little fairy story she's after spinning you, and you fell for it, hook, line and sinker. I can see she has a right eejit made of you...but we all know what she's giving you for your troubles. Her mother was the same, very free with her *favours*.' Julia was dismissive.

'Get out of our home.' Sharif was cut-glass icy.

'Your home, ha! That's a good one.' Julia turned to Carmel and jerked her head at Sharif. 'You're shacked up with this...' She looked Sharif

129

up and down, trying to think of a racist word to describe him.

Sharif moved in so he was almost toe to toe with Julia. His six-foot frame towered over her tiny one. 'Go on, say it. I dare you to show your true colours. You are a twisted, bigoted old harridan, but you can't hurt her any more because she is free, free of both of you.'

Julia pointed her finger at Carmel, each word dripping hatred and vitriol. 'You'll come crawling back, madam, you mark my words, and you'll get the door slammed in your stupid, sponging face. He'll get sick of you when the novelty of a white woman in his bed wears off. He'll get sick of you scrounging off him, and he'll see through you, just as everyone who ever knew you did. You better call off that solicitor, and don't even consider seeking a divorce. That land is Sheehan land and it's staying Sheehan land, do you hear me?'

'That's enough!' Sharif shoved Julia towards the door. 'Get out, you venomous old woman. And as for that brother of yours, tell him he is pathetic and that he will never hear from Carmel again. All dealings from now on are to be through our legal teams, and believe me, ours will be seeking just recompense for the years of unpaid slavery Carmel has done for your family. You can wave goodbye to that little farm. And if you, or he, ever appear here again, I will have you arrested for trespassing, threatening behaviour and assault.' Giving Julia a nudge in the back, he shut the door behind her.

Carmel tried to stay strong, but she dissolved into tears. 'I'm sorry, Sharif. I had no idea she was coming. I was hopeless…'

'Hush, my love, it's all OK. She's gone.' He wrapped his arms around her once more. 'They can't hurt you any more, not really. I know they are awful, but they have no power over you. You're a free agent, free to live where you choose, with whomever you choose. Now, did I go too far, threatening to take the farm? It's your business what you do. We don't need their money, but what they did to you was wrong.'

Carmel giggled a little at the idea of Sharif taking the Sheehan farm. A less likely environment she couldn't imagine for him. 'No, you were right. I'm not going to be bullied any more. Let her stew. I don't want anything to do with the stupid farm, but it's worth it to rattle that old crow. Sharif, I should have told her about us, but I just couldn't. I feel terrible, like I was denying you or something, but I wasn't. I just got such a shock when she turned up out of the blue…'

'It's OK. She knows now anyway. Look, we've sent her packing and hopefully that's the end of it. You weren't exaggerating when you described her. She even looks like the wicked witch in the fairy stories, all thin and pointy features and long greasy hair. She must have left her broomstick outside.' He grinned and seemed happy when she returned it. 'I know she freaked you out by just showing up, and if she ever does that again, just beep me and I'll come, but let's just put her behind us, OK? Marlena buzzed me, saying she looked a bit mad and you seemed shaken – I'm so glad she did. Bill and Julia are from another life, and they've no place in this one.'

'OK.' She smiled weakly. 'I'm just going for a shower. I feel like I need to...I don't know... wash her off me or something.'

'Sure. I'm not going out again, so I'll cook us something, shall I? And try not to picture the dreadful Julia upended on our couch.' He gave her a grin and she smiled back. Maybe it really was going to be OK.

Over dinner, they discussed the party. She didn't tell him about the encounter with Johnson; there had been enough upset for one day.

As they tucked into *dal bhat*, spicy lentils and chapattis, Carmel marvelled at how her taste buds had changed. The first time Sharif made this dish, she thought she'd pass out as it was so spicy, but over time, the flavours had grown on her and now she loved it. Irish food, while very tasty and flavoursome, didn't go big on spices, but she was slowly adapting to her new life.

She made a deliberate effort to keep off the subject of Julia, however disconcerting her sister-in-law's visit had been. The Sheehans had taken up quite enough of her life, and she wasn't going to give them one more second.

'Well, this party is looking more like a gala event every time I overhear something,' Sharif said as she took a second helping of dal. 'I know you want it low-key, and believe me, it's considerably lower in key than what Zane had in mind first day. His plan would have given you a nervous breakdown. I don't care, as I'm dying to show you off to as many people as possible, but you'd have hated it. But they've toned it down, though it's close to impossible to curb Zane's enthusiasm, I think. Even Ivanka and Ivy are powerless in the face of his extreme party planning.'

Carmel sighed. 'I know. It's a waste of time talking to him. I'm imagining *Moulin Rouge*, with me appearing half naked on a swing if he got his way! I was talking to Oscar about it today, before

Julia turned up. He nearly gave me a heart attack when he said he'd have to go home after the strippers.'

Sharif chuckled.

Carmel went on. 'He calmed me down about it anyway. It's just a party, and they're just people we know who want to wish us well. Joe is coming, and he's bringing Luke, Jennifer, Jennifer's husband and their baby. I'm half looking forward to it and half dreading it, to be honest. He texted that he'd told them and they were fine, but what he told them, or what fine really means, I've no idea.'

'I'm sure it means they're fine, happy to know about you and glad for their dad that he's met you,' Sharif said calmly.

'And what if they think, "Who the hell is she, bursting into our lives," or whatever?'

'Carmel, relax. They're coming. That must mean they want to meet you, wish you well, doesn't it?'

'Or kill me. Julia came to visit too, and look how that went.'

The ridiculousness of the entire situation made her laugh. Sharif joined in, and within moments they were both laughing at the hilarity of her monosyllabic ex and his dreadful sister.

CHAPTER 14

'There. You look absolutely stunning.' Ivanka was delighted with her work and smiled as she packed away her brushes, potions and lotions. 'I'll leave you to get dressed, so we'll see you at the party.'

She'd insisted on doing Carmel's make-up. She really was talented, and when she finished, Carmel looked like a more polished and elegant version of herself. The creamy foundation made her skin look flawless. Her blue eyes were accentuated with smoky liner and gold and warm-brown eye shadow, and much to Carmel's initial horror, Ivanka had plucked and shaped Carmel's eyebrows, darkening them slightly. The effect was amazing. Carmel had drawn the line at cherry-red lipstick, opting instead for a coral shade, and the whole effect was, she had to admit, much better than she could ever have imagined. She'd spent the afternoon at the hairdresser's, having her blond wavy hair done in an intricate up style, in which the hair was swept back from her face and twisted loosely behind her head.

Carmel looked warily at her dress once more. It had seemed perfect in the shop, but now she wasn't so sure. It looked expensive, and it was. She'd never worn a silver dress in her life. This one clung in all the right places, according to the saleslady, but Carmel feared it was too much. It was knee-length, but the skirt was split on one side, revealing some recently tanned leg. She pulled it on carefully, trying not to damage her hairstyle. She didn't glance in the mirror until the whole look was complete. The shoes were black patent and high, and would probably be excruciating after an hour or two, but she loved them.

When she was ready, she turned to face the slide robe floor-to-ceiling mirror. Even she had to admit she looked good. *Not bad for a girl nobody wanted*, she thought to herself.

Sharif was going to be home any minute. His clothes were pressed and ready in the walk-in wardrobe. He was wearing a cream suit and an amethyst silk shirt. She'd bought him a lovely mauve handkerchief to complete the outfit. On anyone else, it might look a bit effeminate, but not on Sharif; he was tall and broad, muscular and with no extra fat, and he looked exotic and beautiful when he dressed up. He drew attention wherever he went, and even in a charcoal suit, white shirt and dark tie, which is what he wore most days, he looked handsome. But when he dressed up, he was like a beautiful exotic bird of paradise. She'd told him that a week ago, and he'd laughed so hard.

She tried comparing him to Bill, sweaty and bulging out of his best suit, bought three decades ago; it was impossible. Bill was like an old pig and Sharif like a sleek jaguar.

'Oh, wow! You look amazing. Oh, Carmel, I always thought you were beautiful, but in that dress, you take my breath away.'

She spun around to see Sharif standing at the bedroom door; she had the radio on and didn't hear him come in. 'Is it OK? Not too...'

'Not too sexy, or too glamorous, or too drop-dead gorgeous? Yes, you're all of those, and I'm going to be the proudest man on earth with you on my arm this evening. I'd kiss you, but I'm afraid I'd smudge you...' He just stood and gazed

137

for a moment before he walked past her into the en suite. As he stripped off to shower before dressing, he called, 'By the way, the Kaivalya looks great. I stuck my head around the door as I came up. Zane has been there all day making sure it's perfect. Fresh flowers, sparkly lights, everything. We've brought in extra care assistants to help the patients who want to come to the party to get ready, and the band is tuning up nicely. It's going to be a lovely party, really. Don't worry about a thing.' He stepped into the shower and began singing.

She grinned. He really couldn't carry a tune in a bucket, but she loved to hear him belting out Bruce Springsteen numbers, even if the words were the only way to recognise them in Sharif's off-key rendition.

Despite her jangling nerves, she was kind of looking forward to the evening. She'd never even had a birthday party in her life, so this being her first-ever party in her honour, it was going to be something to remember. She wondered if Joe was there already, and what his children, her possible brother and sister, would be like.

Twenty minutes later, they walked hand in hand across the grounds. They could hear the music, and thankfully it wasn't deafeningly loud, or techno as Zane had suggested – it was a great 1940s swing band. The catering was all in place. Neither of them had had anything to do with the planning. Even if they wanted to, they wouldn't have been allowed to involve themselves in the logistics.

They entered and were immediately greeted by everyone in the room. Wheelchairs were pushed so some of the older residents could shake Sharif's hand or give Carmel a kiss on the cheek. It took twenty minutes for the crowd to disperse and for them to get a drink. A smiling waitress offered them some champagne. They accepted gratefully just as the band leader announced, 'Well, ladies and gentlemen, it appears the guests of honour have arrived. I know you'll all forgive me for deviating from the 1940s vibe for a moment to venture into this number. Sing along, everyone!'

The opening bars of Cliff Richard's 'Congratulations' gave everyone the courage to join in, and soon every guest was singing as Carmel and Sharif danced together in the centre of the room. As she looked into his eyes, he mouthed, 'I love you,' and she kissed him, causing whoops and cheers from the gathered crowd.

Sheila and Kate looked fabulous in matching

outfits. The pair had made a special bird table for Sharif and Carmel's courtyard as a wedding present. It had lovebirds carved on it. Carmel couldn't meet Sharif's eye when they delivered it; he was not a fan of every spare inch of Aashna being covered in bird tables. But there was no curbing their enthusiasm, it would seem. Several hints along the lines of 'how many bird feeders does a place need?' fell on deaf ears.

Tim was there, and Carmel was delighted to see him. They had struck up a friendship in the time since Brian's death, and Carmel knew he was struggling to find purpose in his life without his partner. She was going to ask him if he'd consider telling Joe the true nature of his relationship with Brian. It felt wrong knowing and not saying, and from the way Joe spoke, he wasn't at all judgemental and wouldn't have a bad reaction, Carmel was sure. Tim was in conversation with two other men, one of whom Carmel recognised as a recently admitted patient. Perhaps they knew each other from the local area.

Zane was in his element, accepting compliments on the fabulous party and flirting outrageously with a member of the band. Everyone was dancing and enjoying the fun. The atmosphere was magical.

As their dance drew to a close, the crowd called, 'Speech, speech,' and Sharif took Carmel's hand as he approached the stage. The lead singer handed him the microphone, but Sharif looked questioningly at Carmel.

'Ladies first?' he whispered.

Carmel paled at the thought of addressing all those people, but her need to thank them all and to publicly proclaim her love for Sharif outweighed her terror. 'OK,' she said, trying to control the fluttering in her stomach and the dryness in her mouth. She took the microphone and squeezed it tightly, hardly daring to look up at the sea of expectant faces.

'Em…I've never given a speech, so…em…forgive me if I make a mess of it, but I…I just wanted to say thank you to all of you here to celebrate with me and Sharif tonight. As most of you know, my birth mother, Dolly Mullane, lived here at Aashna House and was great friends with Nadia, Sharif's mum, and indeed Sharif and his dad as well, and somehow, through some strange twist of fate, I find myself here. Not alone that, but I have a life here, friends, a job, a home and someone to love. I never had anything like that before. I want to say thank you from the bottom of my heart to Nadia for welcoming me like a daughter, and to all of you, the patients and staff here at this very special place. To my great friends, Oscar, Ivy, Ivanka. And of course this party wouldn't even be happening, let alone be the amazing extravaganza it is, without Zane, someone both Sharif and I agree is such a vital cog in this machine. I also have to thank one more person. He promised my mother that he wouldn't stop looking for me, even after she died, and he didn't. Despite being so busy here and all his other commitments, he made the time to find me, and he showed me that there was a way to be happy – and more importantly that I was deserving of that, that I should be happy. He brought me here, he mended my broken heart, and he puts up with all my crazy insecurities. He's made sure I'm not going to be a cuckoo any more.' She looked up into his eyes. 'I love you, Sharif, and thank you for rescuing me.'

He hugged her and held her tight as the crowd clapped and cheered. Then the band leader gave him the microphone.

'I don't really know how to follow that, but I'll keep it short. Dolly brought us together. She loved me and she loved Carmel, and as those of you who knew her know, she bore the pain of her daughter's loss every day of her life. But she was great craic, as she, and now my soon-to-be wife, say. I'm the luckiest man in the world to be marrying this funny, kind, clever, beautiful woman. I adore her, as you all know, and I can't wait to marry her. Thank you all for everything you have done for me over the years. Zane and the others have done a spectacular job, so eat up and drink up and enjoy yourselves.'

CHAPTER 15

s they moved away from the stage, Carmel spotted Joe sitting at a table with two others. He smiled and waved at her as she approached them. Sharif got waylaid by some friends, but she didn't mind; she wanted to meet Joe's children on her own anyway.

'Carmel, you look absolutely lovely, really smashing. I can't believe how much like Dolly you are, not that she was ever in such finery when I knew her.' Joe hugged her warmly. Then he released her and stood back, gesturing to the two people behind him. 'Now, this is my son, Luke, and that's my daughter, Jennifer. Lads, this is Carmel.'

Luke was tall, thin and kind of artsy looking. He was in frayed jeans and a grandfather shirt, over the collar of which his brown hair curled. His green eyes were warm and mischievous. He had an earring in one ear, a small silver hoop, and some leather laces around his neck. He stood up. She smelled sandalwood as he gave her a huge bear hug.

'Carmel, it's great to meet you. Welcome to the family. Da is after telling us a bit about you and your background and that, but we're looking forward to getting to know you better.'

'Me too.' Carmel smiled, instantly relaxed with him. Was this guy her little brother? It was mind-blowing if he was.

She then turned to Jennifer, tall like her father and brother, with short dark hair in a pixie cut and blue eyes. She too was dressed very casually, in a tunic and leggings, and her face was perfectly heart-shaped and very pretty. She looked nothing like Joe or Luke. *She must take after her mother,* Carmel guessed.

'Hi, Carmel.' Her voice, though unmistakably Dublin, was gentle. 'Thanks for asking us. It's a lovely party.'

'Thanks for coming. I...well...it means the world to me. Joe said your husband and baby were coming as well?' Carmel wondered where they were.

'Oh, yeah, Damien is staying at the hotel with Ruari – he's asleep by now. If we brought him here, you'd know all about it, I can tell you. He's just crawling, so nothing is safe. I didn't want your first impression of us to by my baby wrecking the place.' She grinned and Carmel re-laxed. They seemed so nice, not out to kill her. As usual, Sharif was right.

'Did you get a drink? Some food?' She was anxious that they be looked after, especially after coming all that way.

'We're grand, fine altogether,' Joe said. 'Now don't feel you have to be minding us all night, right? Go off and enjoy your party. We might slip away soon just to get Jennifer back to Ruari, but maybe we could have lunch tomorrow?' Joe was so understanding and meant what he said, no strings, no pressure.

'I would love that. Why don't you all come round to us? I'll make lunch, and we can have a long chat and get to know each other properly.' Carmel had the invitation issued before she had time to analyse it. Normally, she'd weigh up how likely they were to refuse and probably resist offering for fear of rejection. She smiled hopefully, glad she at least had the guts to ask.

'Sounds great.' Jennifer smiled, putting her head to one side. 'Y'know, I know everyone says you look like your mother, and I'm sure you do, but I can see a bit of McDaid in you as well. Can't you, Luke?'

'Yerra, you know me, Jen, I can't see resemblances in anyone. Sure, people tell me I'm the spit of the da, but I hope not, 'cause he's a banjaxed auld fella, and well, I'm in my prime!' He laughed and nudged his father.

'Go 'way outta that, ya pup. I was in me prime once too, y'know, and I'd have left you in the starting blocks, I can tell ya that.' Joe winked at Carmel as he took a long draught of his pint of Guinness, the barrel of which Zane had shipped from Ireland because British Guinness wasn't the same stuff at all.

'That's great. I'll ask Nadia as well – that's Sharif's mum. She's lovely. I'm really looking forward to it.'

'Me too.' Joe sounded so sincere, and she warmed under his gaze. 'Now, go off and be chatting to all these people who've come to see you, and we'll see you tomorrow, OK? Have a great night, pet.' He put his arm around her protectively for a moment, and Carmel felt five years old again. Except this was a sensation she'd never had as a five-year-old. She trusted this man, and she just knew, on some deep level, that he was a good person.

Carmel kissed Joe on the cheek and went off to mingle. As she moved around the party, people complimenting her on how lovely she looked stopped her several times, then she was enveloped in a group hug by Zane, Ivanka, Ivy and Oscar. They dragged her out onto the dance floor, and she was soon bopping away to 'Don't Sit Under the Apple Tree' with her friends. Everyone was having a great time. The canapés being circulated by the waiting staff were delicious. She spoke to patients and their families, met Oscar's partner, Caroline, who was just like him, so chilled out and happy, and Zane insisted on being introduced to Luke, despite Carmel saying she didn't think he was gay.

'With all due what's it, Carmel darlin', I think I'm the better judge of that sort of thing.' He winked and dragged her back to Joe and his children.

Carmel introduced them and went to look for Sharif; she hadn't seen him since the speeches over forty minutes earlier. Everyone seemed to be in high spirits, and the music complemented nicely the lively buzz of chat in the room. With Sharif being so tall and with his distinctive hair, she could nearly always spot him in a crowd, but as she scanned the room, he wasn't to be seen. Hoping nobody would notice, she stepped out into the corridor joining the Kaivalya to the main building. The silence was instantaneous. All the doors in Aashna House were soundproof, so the party noise didn't spill out. Perhaps he'd got a call about a patient, she thought. She would just go to reception and check if he'd been called. Marlena was at the party, as were most of the regular staff, so there were several temporary and agency staff on duty. Sharif probably just wanted to check everything was OK.

Reception was empty – most of the patients would be in bed by now – and a young man, presumably from the temp agency, was on the desk.

'May I help, madam?' he asked politely.

'Yes, I'm em…I'm Carmel, I work here. I was just looking for Dr Khan. Has he been called to a patient?'

The young man seemed uncomfortable. 'Well, em, Dr Khan is with somebody at the moment. Perhaps I can give him a message for you?'

'A patient?' Carmel sensed some reticence in the man's answer.

'No, ma'am, not a patient, a family member, but I'm sure if you leave a message, I'll make sure he gets it...'

They both turned on hearing raised voices coming from the office behind the reception desk. Suddenly, the door burst open and Derek Johnson emerged. 'Well, let's see what my solicitor has to say about you partying while my poor mother lay in her own filth, half starved. I've got photos, so don't even try to deny it! You're a crook and a criminal, and I'll see you pay for this! Mark my words, you will pay...' He barged past Carmel and out into the night.

Through the open door, Carmel could see Sharif standing behind the desk in the office. Quickly, she went to him.

'Madam, if you could just wait...' the receptionist began. He'd clearly been given instructions not to disturb the doctor.

'It's OK. Thanks, but it's fine.' She went into the office and closed the door. 'What on earth was all that about?' Carmel had never seen Sharif so shaken.

He gazed at Carmel, then shook his head. 'He's claiming that when he came in to see his mother this evening, she was lying in sheets covered in excrement and blood, that she hadn't been fed, that she was in mental and physical distress. And somehow he has photos to back up his claim.' He sat down heavily in the seat.

'But that's simply not true!' Carmel was appalled. 'I mean, it just couldn't be. Mrs Johnson was fine when I popped in this afternoon. She'd just had her lunch. They were clearing it away when I arrived. I even remarked to her about the cottage pie, how I'd had it for lunch as well and how delicious it was. She smiled, the way she does, you know, and seemed to understand. There's no way that what he is claiming has a grain of truth.'

Sharif sighed deeply. 'I know that and you know that, but it's our word against his, and he's got photographs on his phone. I've seen them. She's sitting in a wet, dirty bed, and she's crying. It doesn't matter what the truth is – what matters is how it looks. He's threatening to take it legal, or go to the papers with his so-called evidence. He could destroy us, destroy me.' He ran his hand over his jaw.

'But all the staff here, we'd all testify –'

He interrupted her. 'And what would they say? Of course the staff of the private clinic would back it up – they don't want to be found to be professionally negligent either. No, Carmel, I don't know what to do, but fighting him is probably not the answer. I mentioned him to David Harrison – you know, the solicitor you're dealing with as well – the last time he was shooting his mouth off. His advice at the time was to ship Mrs Johnson out. He said that, in his experience, it never ended well when someone was making claims against doctors. Fighting it in court can take years, and it's cripplingly expensive and ultimately fruitless because the reputational damage is already done.'

'But you didn't move her because you promised her you'd take care of her. Oh, Sharif...' She went to hug him, and together they stood in the quiet office, clinging to each other.

After several moments had passed, he broke the silence. 'We'd better get back to the party.'

'I suppose so.' She sighed. 'It's honestly the last thing on earth I feel like doing now. But you're right. They've gone to so much trouble, and we've all those people yet to speak to.'

'Yes. I'm just going to check on Mrs Johnson, see what on earth is going on, and I'll join you then. Can you just say I've been called to a patient?'

'Of course. Do you want me to come with you?'

'No, better one of us is at the party at least. I'll see her and talk to the night staff. He picked tonight on purpose because of all the agency staff. He's taken some pictures of us dancing and the party too – he must have been outside or something – so despite what we know, it looks bad. It's not a coincidence he chose tonight. He's done his homework. Everyone here watches out for him, hovers around when he's in, but these agency people wouldn't have known.'

They smiled goodnight at the young man on reception. Sharif instructed him to beep him if there was anything unusual happening, and they walked hand in hand down the corridor.

'It's going to be OK, Sharif. We can survive this. I don't know how, but you can't be punished for being kind. The universe doesn't work that way.'

He squeezed her hand. 'I'd love to think you're right, my love, but I'm not that confident. I've seen so many malpractice cases, especially in recent years. A college friend of mine was sued for sexually harassing a patient when the truth was the patient had a crush on him. He rejected her, and she took it very personally. She said he made a pass at her in the examination room when she was undressed, when the complete opposite was the case. I'm not saying to doesn't happen, I know it does, but in this case it was a complete lie, but the truth didn't matter, and the result was the loss of his practice, the near collapse of his marriage and the alienation of his kids. She was very convincing. It was proved later to be totally fabricated, but the damage was done. More often than not, doctors settle. Even if there's no truth in it whatsoever. And I think that's what Johnson is after – money.'

'But that's blackmail! He can't get away with that surely?' Carmel was so upset at the thought of someone hurting Sharif.

He shrugged and sighed heavily. 'No, maybe, I don't know. Look, you go back. The last thing we need is a search party or for anyone to know about this until I figure it out myself.'

'All right, we'll talk later.' She stood on her tiptoes and kissed him once they reached Mrs Johnson's room, and he gave her a watery smile.

CHAPTER 16

'What a lovely party last night.' Nadia was her usual effusive self as she arrived at the apartment for lunch the next day, and she gave Carmel and Sharif each a warm embrace. 'I've made carrot *halwa* for dessert, Sharif – I know how much you love it!'

Joe and the family had yet to arrive. Jennifer was bringing Damien and Ruari, so they'd have to squeeze up. Sharif had called maintenance for another table and more chairs, and Nadia was busy decorating the long table beautifully with candles, flowers and ornaments.

Sharif had been up since dawn. They'd talked long into the night once all the guests had gone and decided they would have to address all the staff on Monday morning, explain what was happening and ask them if they knew anything. Carmel was devastated for Sharif, his whole life's work threatened by some horrible greedy man, but she was glad he could share his worries with her. The way he spoke – we will do this, we will say that – made her feel like an intrinsic part of Aashna House, and her desire to defend it and Sharif was intense. That Johnson man could not be allowed to win. It was almost four in the morning when she eventually fell asleep.

Sharif must not have slept at all because he had the entire meal ready when she woke.

'I couldn't sleep anyway, so I thought I might as well keep busy. I made *aloo gosht* with naan – I hope they'll like it. It has potatoes in it.' He smiled. It was a running joke of theirs that potatoes would have to be cooked every day, just as Bill demanded.

'I'm sure they will. It's not too spicy, is it?' She was a little worried. While she was getting used to the chilli peppers he put in every dish and quite enjoyed the flavours now, she was nowhere near being able to eat what Sharif and Nadia could in terms of hot, spicy food. She suspected Joe might be the same.

'I don't think so. I tried it, and to me it tastes bland, so it's probably about right for the Irish palate. Here, try.' He offered her a spoon from the pot.

The glistening sauce dripped from the piece of lamb he offered her. She tasted it, and while it was certainly on the spicy side, she could eat it without feeling the need to run her head under a tap. She hoped Joe could handle it. She was less concerned about Luke, Jennifer and Damien. Dublin had become so multicultural in the past decade, everyone was used to food from all around the world. The baby, Ruari, was seven months, so Sharif had bought some little yoghurts and fruit purees when he shopped for the meal earlier in case Jennifer needed something to feed him.

The shock from the previous night and her worry about Sharif had totally replaced her nerves at meeting the family properly. They'd seemed so nice, she was sure it was going to go well. She heard a cab pull up outside and went out to greet them. Joe was in the front, and Luke, Damien, Jennifer and the baby tumbled out of the back, complete with buggies and bags of all descriptions.

'I'm sorry, Carmel. We look like we're moving

in, I know. I honestly don't know how one small baby needs so much stuff, but it seems he does.' Jennifer laughed as she gave Carmel a one-armed hug, a gorgeous Ruari lodged on her other hip. The baby looked just like his father, dark haired and stocky.

Luke and Damien carried the rest of the things inside, and Sharif directed them to the spare bedroom. The sudden cacophony of chat and laughter seemed to defuse the sense of impending doom they were both feeling.

'Now so, Ruari, this is Carmel. Carmel, meet Ruari.' Jennifer waved the baby's fat little hand in her direction, and his face cracked into a wide gummy grin.

He was adorable, and Carmel felt a pang. How lucky Jennifer was to have this little baby in her life. 'Hello, Ruari! How lovely to meet you. And what a handsome little man you are, yes you are. Oh, Jennifer, he's just gorgeous.'

Damien piped up from behind Jennifer. 'Ah, thanks, I have my moments.'

Carmel laughed and instantly liked him. 'I meant the baby.' She chuckled. She stuck out her hand. 'I'm Carmel. Lovely to meet you, Damien, thanks for coming. Oh, and thanks for doing the honours last night so Jennifer could come to the party.'

He grinned and Carmel could see how his smile was reflected exactly in Ruari's. 'Not a bother. Jen says it's not babysitting when it's your own kid – parenting or something she calls it!'

Jennifer gave him a good-natured thump on the arm. 'Now that he's taking bottles, there'll be much more of that, I can tell you, so you better get used to it. He got away with murder the last few months. Do you know I overheard him telling his mam how Ruari never wakes at night? I couldn't believe my ears! Because I can tell you, there's only one person in our house who doesn't wake at night, and it sure as anything isn't Ruari.'

Nadia was deep in chat with Joe, and Luke and Sharif were joking about football. Sharif was a Luton Town fan, despite their lowly status, and he'd been going to games since he was a child. Luke was a Liverpool supporter, so the inevitable teasing began. Carmel had no idea what they were on about, but she was happy to see Sharif relax and relieved that the McDaids blended seamlessly into the gathering.

The food went down a treat. It turned out that Joe lived in England for a period during the '60s when there was no work at home and had developed quite a taste for Asian cuisine.

'I used to share a flat with a lad from Bangalore – we were working together in a big abattoir out near Finsbury. The flat was absolutely tiny, but we didn't mind. I remember him telling me how tightly squeezed in they were back where he came from, and I explained to him about being one of six in a two-bed terraced house in Kilmainham, so we got on grand. We'd take turns cooking – couldn't afford to eat out or anything like that. At the start, everything he made used to blow the head off me, so it would, but after a while, I got into it. Cardamom and garam masala and all sorts, and then being in the abattoir, we had access to the end cuts if we wanted them. The way he cooked the meat, slowly and with loads of spices, it kind of tenderised it. We lived like kings and never spent a shilling. I used to make these spice rubs then, when I had my own butcher shop, and people used to go mad for them, all taught to me by my friend Rahul.'

The table erupted in questions at the image of Joe and his Bangalore friend eating together every night in cramped quarters.

'What happened to him?' Nadia asked, fascinated.

'He went back to Bangalore to marry some girl his mother picked out or something. He was none too pleased, I can tell you, but Rahul's mammy called and Rahul did as he was told.' Joe grinned.

Carmel stole a glance at Sharif. He was engaged with everything, though undoubtedly the situation with Derek Johnson couldn't be too far from his mind. She just sat back and observed everyone chatting and joking with each other. Joe and Nadia were getting on famously, each telling stories of Dolly. Luke was playing on the floor with Ruari, and Sharif, Jennifer and Damien were discussing the situation in the North of Ireland. It struck her that even though these people were from very different cultures, they had so much in common. She'd never had more than a passing acquaintance with anyone other than native-born Irish before coming to England and was still amazed that the worries, joys and preoccupations of people she knew back in Ireland were replicated here, no matter what colour or religion people were.

Ivanka was worried about her elderly parents back in Stockholm. Her dad had Parkinson's, and though they were wealthy, she felt guilty about not being there. Zane was openly gay, but his dad was a macho West Indian and couldn't accept his son's sexuality. Ivy's daughter was in the middle of a bitter divorce, and Ivy was worried about her and her grandkids. And Nadia was dreading a visit from her very pernickety sister, who was insisting on coming from Karachi to criticise, according to Nadia.

CHAPTER 17

*T*he two families blended so effortlessly. *Maybe that's what having a family means,* Carmel thought, *that you aren't a lone entity in the world, that there is strength in numbers so you can explore the world and other people with a bit more confidence.* Then something occurred to her: These people didn't just belong to each other; they kind of belonged to her as well. In fact, she was the common denominator. She had never before had a family to call her own, and yet, as she looked around at Nadia, Joe, Jennifer, Luke, Damien, Ruari and, of course, her darling Sharif, she realised that for the first time ever, she was part of a family. Tears came unbidden, and she decided to start clearing plates rather than make a total show of herself in front of everyone.

Immediately everyone tried to help, but Jennifer stopped them. 'I'll help Carmel and you all sit here. You'll only be in the way if we all try to do it. Why don't we clear up and then the men can take over coffee and desserts, right?'

There was general agreement.

'Well, I was slaving over a hot –' Luke began, with a wink at Carmel.

'Visa card,' Jennifer finished for her brother. 'Don't try to make out that you baked that, Luke.' She nodded in the direction of the pie they'd brought, along with wine and chocolate and a lovely bunch of flowers. 'Don't you know the trick? If you want it to look homemade, you need to take it out of the box, pop it on a plate of your own and bash the sides up a bit. Those perfectly round cakes are a dead giveaway.'

'Ah, Jen, do tell me that lovely apple tart you feed me when I go round to your house is made by your own fair hands?' Joe's mock anguish caused them all to chuckle.

'Sorry, Dad, Tesco's all the way!' She smiled sweetly and kissed him on the cheek.

'What a disappointment you've turned out to be,' he said, pretending to be wounded. 'Carmel, how about you? You wouldn't pawn off some mass-produced auld muck on me, now, would you? I bet if you made an apple tart, it would be better than Jennifer's, from this day forward to be called Tesco's.'

Carmel smiled weakly and went to the kitchen. She stood at the sink, gripping the cold stainless steel. She didn't dare catch Jennifer's eye. She figured the other woman must be devastated to hear her father suggest that Carmel could be a better daughter than her. Carmel knew Joe was only joking, but still, Jennifer had had her father's undiluted adoration all her life. She was probably either hurt or mad that Joe would say such a thing, and Carmel felt guilty for being the cause of that.

Jennifer landed a pile of dirty plates on the worktop and started scraping the scraps into the bin. Carmel couldn't make eye contact. Perhaps she should say something, anything, to show Jennifer that she wasn't trying to muscle in.

'Your tableware is beautiful. Where did you get it? It reminds me of the stuff my granny had when I was small, so delicate.' Nothing in Jennifer's tone suggested the outrage she must be feeling.

Carmel dared raise her eyes, and she was

greeted by Jennifer's open, happy face. 'Em… Nadia gave them to us. They were actually my mother's, apparently, but she gave the set to Nadia when she was dying. She saved up to buy all the different pieces.' Carmel gently placed each one into the dishwasher.

'It must be so hard for you, to be here in the place where she was, but too late to have met her. My mam died, but I have loads of memories, and even though I really miss her and some days it's harder than others, I can picture her clearly, hear her voice. I don't know – it doesn't feel so lonely, I suppose.'

The two women worked easily together, clearing the many plates and serving bowls. Carmel was glad of the distraction. Amazingly, Jennifer didn't seem at all put out by the apple tart remark.

'Well, it is, but I never knew her, and to be honest, growing up, I tried not to think too much about who my mother was. I believed she had me and chose for whatever reason not to keep me, and that was all there was to it really. It wasn't until I met Sharif that she became a real person to me. But yeah, hearing Nadia and Sharif talking about her, and now your dad, it does make me wish all the time that I could have met her.'

Jennifer found a dishwashing tablet and placed it in the machine, getting it going. She leaned on the worktop and took a sip of her wine. 'He was so happy you turned up, you know. When he came home from Brian's funeral, he texted from the airport to say he needed to talk to us. We didn't come over because Ruari was too small to fly with at that stage, and Luke couldn't go because he was in Spain on a case.' She noted Carmel's look of surprise. 'Oh, he didn't tell you? He's a Guard. Well, more special branch, like a detective. Don't be fooled by the homeless hippie look – he's a smart cookie, my brother. Not much gets past him.'

Of all the professions Carmel could have imagined for Luke, a policeman would have been the very last. He looked like a student.

'Anyway,' Jennifer went on, 'Dad came back, and one night he took me and Luke out to dinner and told us about you. Hearing him talk about your mam... We'd never seen him like that before. Like, he loved my mam, no doubt about it, but even she told me that she wasn't his first love. Everyone round them knew how gutted he was when Dolly left. My mam told me that the night before their wedding, she went round to Dad's house and asked him straight out if he was still in love with Dolly, and if he was, then he shouldn't marry her. He told her the truth, that a bit of him would always love Dolly but that she was gone and he'd waited long enough for her to come back and it was clear she wasn't going to. He told her that he wanted to marry her and that he'd be faithful and loving towards her till the day one of them died. So she accepted that, and they really did have a great marriage.' Jennifer's voice cracked, betraying how much she still missed her mother.

'I'm glad.' Carmel wondered if she should touch her or hug her or something, but she didn't know how Jennifer would take that so she didn't. 'He's such a nice man – he deserves to be happy.' Carmel didn't really know what else to say. Had Joe told Jennifer that he was Carmel's father? Or had he told them about the ambiguity, and if so, did they know the details? She wished she'd had a chance to speak to Joe on his own before the lunch, but it was too late for that now.

'What are you thinking about the whole thing?' Jennifer asked. 'It must be incredibly weird for you...suddenly finding a family you never knew you had?'

'It is,' Carmel answered honestly. 'Really

strange, but in a nice way. I don't know. I'm still just processing it all, I suppose.'

'Are you going to have the test?' There it was, the blunt question. The tone was gentle, but the question was definitely direct.

Carmel had lived a life where nobody said anything of any consequence, or at least not to her, and so when people were forthright or inquisitive, she found herself at a bit of a loss. 'Do you think I should?' Carmel was surprised at herself for meeting such a blunt question with one of her own.

Jennifer smiled and sighed. 'I don't know, honestly I don't. I've gone over this and over it. Dad wants you to be his daughter, and he believes you are. I'm just thinking, are you better off just assuming that you are, if it's what you both want, rather than risk finding out that you're not his biological child and ruining everything? Like, I think you are. I can see a resemblance even, not so much to Dad but to my aunties and cousins. But if your dad is just some random bloke Dolly was with some time, then won't it hurt both of you?'

So, Carmel was relieved to note, Joe hadn't told them about the grandfather. He must just have said that maybe Dolly had a relationship or something with someone else. Though Carmel knew logically Dolly hadn't done anything wrong, as Sharif was constantly pointing out, she was delighted that Jennifer and Luke didn't know the truth. 'And what about you? How would you feel about it?' Carmel tried to keep her voice light, but she was sure Jennifer could sense her anxiety from across the small kitchen.

'I'd love it,' Jennifer said without hesitation. 'I've always wanted a sister. I mean, I'm probably past the robbing your clothes and make-up phase, but it would be lovely just to have a sister, y'-know? And for Ruari to have an auntie?' Her voice cracked with emotion and she reddened, clearly embarrassed.

Carmel crossed the kitchen and embraced her, all thoughts of how awkward it could be for-gotten. 'Do I know? Oh yes, I know. I'd love a sister too.'

Releasing her, Jennifer asked, 'So where does that leave us? We want you in our family, and we think you are our sister. We can find out for sure or leave well enough alone – what do you think?'

They were interrupted by Sharif arriving in the kitchen to make coffee. Nadia was busy un-wrapping her *halwa* to appreciative sounds, and Luke was making a great show of battering the outsides of the chocolate cream pie he'd bought. Jennifer accepted the little yoghurts that Sharif had bought for Ruari, exclaiming that they were his favourite, and Sharif gave her a squeeze. Carmel wondered if she knew before this that it was possible to be this happy.

After dessert, there was coffee and delicious Baileys Irish Cream chocolates, which everyone said they couldn't possibly touch because they were so full, but they still managed to polish off almost the entire box.

Sharif tapped his glass. The room became instantly quiet; even little Ruari rested peacefully in Jennifer's arms.

'I'm not much of a man for speeches normally, but there is something I want to tell you all. Seeing everyone here today, so relaxed and happy in each other's company, it feels like we are family already. Carmel and I can't make any plans for our wedding until she can get a divorce, but as soon as she does, we will be getting married, and I know I speak for her too when I say we would love it if you'd join us on that day.'

CHAPTER 18

*J*oe was sitting beside Carmel, and he put his arm around her shoulders. She turned to him and smiled. He winked at her and her heart melted. She realised now, for sure, she wanted this man in her life. But maybe Jennifer was right. What would a DNA test prove? If it was positive and he was her father, then they were exactly where they were now, and if not... Well, if not, who knew what anyone would feel?

'The second thing is something to do with the clinic,' Sharif continued. 'I know I've only just met you, and normally I am a very private person on such issues, but Carmel and I are going to need your support in the coming months. In a nutshell, I am being threatened with a malpractice suit.' Even saying the words out loud caused him pain; Carmel could see it.

Nadia paled; she knew how serious this was. 'By whom? That's ridiculous! You are the most diligent, conscientious...'

Sharif smiled as he saw the mother lioness emerge, protecting her cub. '*Ammi*, I know you think that, and I will, of course, fight this if I can, but basically a patient suffering from dementia was photographed by her son in soiled, wet sheets, and he is claiming that on a regular basis, we neglect her.'

'But, Sharif, my darling...how can he say such a thing? It's that Derek Johnson, isn't it? I knew he couldn't be trusted. You are letting his mother stay here, with top facilities, for nothing just because she asked you to, and now this is how he repays you?'

Sharif had never told Carmel that Mrs Johnson wasn't a paying patient, but she'd suspected. That made the whole thing so much worse.

'That's irrelevant. The thing is, it's not true. He must have brought those sheets in and put them on the bed and then photographed her. In the pictures he showed me, her nightgown was all stained and her hair very dishevelled, as well as there were dirty sheets and rubbish all over the room. There was even a full ashtray. He clearly staged the whole thing. But as I explained to Carmel, malpractice suits are notoriously difficult and costly to fight, and often the damage is actually done by the suspicion anyway. Most of the time, doctors settle. I've spoken to my solicitor and he's put me on to a legal team that specialises in this sort of thing, but their advice is going to be to settle, I would imagine.'

Carmel placed her hand over his as he sat down.

Joe was the first to speak. 'Sharif, I don't know anything about you really, but from what my brother said about this place, I know that man is lying. Surely he can't just come up with a load of rubbish like that and expect to get away with it?'

'Well, it seems he can. It's not fair, but then... life isn't fair sometimes. Anyway, there you have it. We'll need your support, as I said, and I just thought it was better to tell you what was going on. It might even wind up in the papers, so I'd rather you heard it from us. I know I don't need to say this, but I'd appreciate it if you kept this to yourselves.'

'Of course. That's awful,' Jennifer said. She

and Luke both reached out for Carmel's hand at the same time, and for an instant, she felt a sibling connection.

'Now, I don't want this to spoil our lovely day, so let's not talk about it any more, but I wanted you all to know. It will all work itself out, I'm sure.' Sharif smiled with a confidence Carmel knew he didn't feel, but he was right; there was no point in dwelling on it.

'So how long are you all staying around?' Carmel hoped she'd have some time with them on her own before they went back to Ireland.

'Well, myself, Damien, Luke and the little prince here are going back tomorrow, but I think Dad is staying around for a few days, aren't you?' Jennifer must have known her father was a little nervous, afraid of outstaying his welcome, so she was encouraging.

Carmel jumped in right away. 'Oh, that's wonderful. I'm really sorry you guys are going back so soon, but I know how it is with work and everything, and I'm so grateful that you came over. Really, travelling with Ruari and everything, it's meant the world to us, and especially to me. And maybe we can spend some time together, Joe, over the next few days? That's if the boss will give me the time off. He's a bit of a tyrant.' She winked at Sharif.

'Somehow, Carmel, I think you have him wrapped around your little finger.' Joe looked relieved that she was pleased.

'She certainly does, Joe. I'm a slave to her whims.' Sharif pretended to be mournful.

'Hey, say if this is a bad idea now,' Damien said, 'but how about if myself and Joe mind the small lad and let Jennifer, Luke and Carmel go out for a drink or something? We're all going back tomorrow and maybe...' He got embarrassed then, clearly unsure of how to finish because nobody had yet said anything about the situation of Carmel's parentage.

'I'd love that. If it suits you two?' Carmel knew Jennifer was anxious to welcome her, but she'd love to talk properly to Luke as well. The family lunch was wonderful, but it didn't allow for any real conversation about the future.

'Perfect,' said Sharif. 'Now, I need to get over to the clinic, check on everyone, so I'll take my leave of you all. We had a lovely time. Thank you so much for coming, and please come over again soon.' Sharif picked up his keys and made for the door.

'Or you could come to visit us?' Luke grinned.

'Maybe. Dublin was where we met, so maybe we could go back for a visit sometime?' Sharif knew that Carmel had no desire to ever return to Ireland, but maybe a family of her own over there would be enough of a lure.

'Maybe,' Carmel responded.

'Don't worry about clearing up. I'll do it when I get back.' And Sharif was gone.

Nadia and Joe began removing the dessert plates and the glasses, and Damien took Ruari off to change him into his pyjamas.

'Right, Carmel, show us the highlights of this bit of the urban sprawl,' Luke joked as he shrugged on his jacket.

'Well, we are just a teeny bit too far out to be considered urban anything, but we could go in to London if you like, up the West End or some-thing, or we could just stay around here? What-ever you two would like.'

'Well' – Jennifer checked her hair in the mirror – 'maybe this single brother of ours is looking for a bit more action than a night with his sisters, but I'm happy to stay local.' She smiled, and Carmel coloured at the casual way she'd dropped in the word 'sisters'.

'What more could a fella want? I already had one nagging sister, now it seems I've got two.

Brilliant.' He threw his eyes heavenward and, with a martyred sigh, offered them an arm each. 'Right, you, where are you taking us?'

Carmel thought quickly. 'I'm not much of a pub goer, but my friends Zane and Ivanka hang out at the Dog and Duck and say it's fun. We go there for lunch some days. So will we try there? We can walk – it's about twenty minutes – or we can call a cab?'

'Oh, let's walk. I'm stuffed after that lunch. I could do with some exercise.' Jennifer patted her belly.

Luke looked doubtfully at his sister's high boots. 'Are you going to be able to walk in those and not be whining after three minutes? You know what you're like, and I'm not carrying you!'

'Hmm, good point.' Jennifer looked down ruefully.

'What size are you? I can lend you a pair of pumps?'

Jennifer looked at Carmel and grinned. 'Maybe it's not too late after all to be borrowing your stuff! I'm a six?'

'Me too. Come into the bedroom and see what you'd like.'

'Here we go,' Luke moaned dramatically. 'One

pair of shoes, Jen, and only to borrow. A thirty-second decision, not a half an hour, OK?'

'Yeah, yeah, whatever.' She punched him playfully on the shoulder.

Five minutes later, Jennifer emerged wearing a pair of flat ballet pumps and a cream and gold jacket of Carmel's. 'I love this jacket – it's so unusual,' she said.

'Ivy gave it to me. Someone bought it for her as a present, but she's in her sixties and she felt ridiculous in it. Keep it if you like.'

'I couldn't do that – it's yours.'

'And now it's yours. I like the idea of you having it. You can think of me when you wear it.'

'OK, now that the fashion show is over, can we please get going? One sister was bad enough...' Luke grinned, then kissed Nadia on the cheek and gave his dad a hug.

Jennifer did the same and Carmel followed their lead. She was never quite sure what to do in these situations. Certainly, as a child, there was no physical contact at all, and during her years with Bill, it was kept to an absolute minimum. The twins would give her a peck on the cheek when they arrived and left, and she shook hands with people when it was time to show the sign of peace at Mass, but apart from that, she wasn't really touched by anyone. Over here, she was constantly being hugged and kissed by Sharif, friends, Nadia. And while it was lovely, she was always a little unsure about what she should do.

'Be careful and mind each other,' Joe called as they closed the door behind them.

'So tell us more about this Johnson fella.'

Carmel was surprised at Luke's interest, but she told him all she knew.

'So he just rocks up out of the blue and says he's her son and starts all this trouble?'

Carmel remembered that Luke was a detective and assumed that's where his interest lay. 'Well, we've no reason to believe he's not her son, but yeah, that's more or less it. Poor Sharif. It's killing him inside, though he doesn't let on. He's so conscientious that he would never allow anything like that to happen. And Johnson took the photos the same night as the party, so it looks like we were having a great time while this poor lady was being neglected. I just wish there was something I could do.'

'Well, just be there for him, I suppose – y'-know, what you're doing. Imagine if he didn't have you?' Jennifer said kindly.

'Well, I hope I'm being some use, but to be honest, I doubt it. I approached the horrible man, that Johnson, you know, the other day in the car park, and he was so aggressive and rude. Apparently, he hates Paddies and Pakis, so in his eyes Sharif and I are both equally bad. You should see him and his car, filthy, smelly, and I just can't believe that he's suddenly the caring son. Sharif has known Mrs Johnson for years, and the son never featured at all. None of it fits. I haven't told Sharif that I spoke to him. Maybe I should? I just wanted to help him, but what if I've made things worse? Sharif thinks he'll look for money.'

'I doubt that.' Luke was circumspect. 'He sounds like a right piece of work. If you want me to, I could ask someone I know at Scotland Yard to run a check on him? If we knew a bit more about him, then it could help find a way to deal with him?'

Carmel felt so touched at Luke's offer to help and the way he seemed to see it as a collective problem, not just Sharif's.

'I'll speak to Sharif, see what he says. Thanks so much, Luke. You don't really need this in your life I'm sure, but we really appreciate it.'

'I deal with criminals all day, every day. In general, they are cowards under all the bravado and nearly always have something to hide. Find that, and you have leverage. Simple really, when you know how!' He winked.

'Do you think he's a criminal?' Carmel asked, aghast.

'Well' – Luke ticked the points off on his fingers – 'so far, he's falsified evidence, made unfounded accusations and made racist remarks. We also think he's about to try to blackmail you guys, and he's distressed his poor old mother for his own nefarious ends. Let's just say I wouldn't be stunned if it turns out he has a record. Normal, law-abiding people just don't do things like that.'

'And you could find that out for us?' Carmel asked.

'I would imagine so. Yeah.'

CHAPTER 19

Carmel glanced at Luke and wondered if the whole student look wasn't a sort of disguise. He came across as jokey and very much the baby brother when he was goofing around with the family, but now that he was in business mode, he was focused and professional.

'If we can help in any way, Carmel,' Jennifer added, 'we will. You've been through enough in your life – you deserve a break. And it's just so unfair that now that you and Sharif have found each other and your story with your parents is just starting to emerge, that you have to deal with this awful man and his horrible threats.' Jennifer was sincere; Carmel just knew it.

'You have no idea what it means to me to hear

you say that, both of you,' she replied. 'Seriously, I was terrified before the party that you were coming over to tell me to back off, to leave your dad alone. And I wouldn't have blamed you. But you're both so easy to talk to. I don't know much about how families work because the whole thing was a bit of a mystery to me – I learned everything about relationships from TV soaps. To be honest, I thought it was always fraught. But seeing Sharif and Nadia together, and Joe and you lot, it all seems so easy. I can't believe I'm actually in one, a real proper family. I just sat and watched you all over lunch, talking, eating, laughing, and I felt such awe. And then I realised I was actually part of it, not outside looking in, the way I have been all my life. I know that sounds tragic, but honestly, I was breathing in and out and going through the motions, but I wasn't living, not really.'

'What was Trinity House like?' Luke asked as they walked along. In some ways, Carmel realised, it was easier to talk properly when walking, eyes straight ahead.

'OK. Like, I wasn't abused or anything. That's the first thing everyone thinks these days when they hear I was reared in care. We went to the local school, and I remember I used to dread when there would be a note to go home to have signed for different things. Each one of the normal kids would be given a note, and then when it came to us, the kids from Trinity, they'd say, "Ye don't need to take one. It's been sent." I used to cringe with shame. My first communion, confirmation, all of that, it was the same. We went with the others to the church – they even found dresses or whatever for us – but no photos, no family lunch, no cash from your aunties and uncles. The usual stuff kids think about, I suppose. So it was lonely and embarrassing and empty, but they weren't cruel.'

'But no love?' Jennifer asked.

'No,' Carmel conceded. 'Nothing like that.'

'And you must have been wondering why you weren't adopted?'

Carmel knew now that Jennifer and Luke didn't have the full story, so she couldn't explain about the order Joe's father had made. 'I just supposed that nobody wanted me. Like, once you go past four or five, it's almost impossible anyway. People really only want babies, so I remember on my seventh birthday deciding I wasn't going to think about that any more. It wasn't going to happen and that was that.'

Luke put his arm around her and gave her a

squeeze. 'Is that why you married that fella from down the country?'

Carmel shrugged. 'I suppose so. I was well over eighteen, and it was time to be out of care. And well, I'd nowhere else to go. I didn't have any qualifications. I got my Leaving Cert, but without a proper address or some experience, I couldn't even get a job in a shop. I could sew, and I used to make clothes for the kids in Trinity or adjust the stuff out of the charity bags that were dropped in, but there wasn't any need for that any more. I thought that because Bill had kids and their mother had died, that they'd need me. I used to look after the little ones at Trinity House, and I like kids, so I just thought... Well, anyway, they didn't need me or want me, as it turned out. I think Bill only got married to keep his awful sister out of his house, and a bit for the girls, I suppose, but then when they didn't want me, it was all kind of pointless.'

'How old were they?' Jennifer was clearly upset at such cruelty.

'Oh, they were only nine when Bill and I got married, but Julia kind of dominated them.'

'Oh, she's the one that showed up the other day? She sounds like a right wagon.' Luke had heard from Sharif about the dreadful Julia.

'Oh, she's a piece of work all right. Sharif says she looks like a witch in a storybook, all pointy.' Carmel chuckled.

'And did you not want to have a child with your man?' Luke was so direct. It must have been the policeman in him, but Carmel found that she didn't mind.

'This is going to sound mad, but we never actually…well, you know. He was still married in his head to his dead wife, and so he never touched me.' Carmel couldn't believe she was admitting this to them, but somehow it felt safe.

'Are you serious?' Luke was incredulous, and Jennifer had tears in her eyes.

'And you're so gorgeous, and he never wanted… Oh, Carmel, you poor thing, that must have been so hard…' Jennifer was trying her best to hold it together, Carmel could see, but it was impossible.

Once again, Carmel was surprised at the impact of her story. Each time she told it, first to Sharif, then Nadia, and bit by bit to her new friends, she tried to make it sound less like a bad melodrama, but it always had the same impact.

Luke stopped walking and drew both of them into his embrace. 'Come on now, we're supposed to be celebrating, so let's try to focus on that, eh?

They're out of your life now – well, almost, just the divorce to get sorted, and then you've got all sorts of options.'

The pub was half full, and there was a nice buzz of conversation. Carmel went to the bar, dismissing Luke's efforts to buy the first round.

'What can I get you, love?' the barman asked as Luke and Jennifer went to sit down.

'I'll have a gin and tonic please and a glass of red for my sister and a pint of bitter for my brother.'

The barman looked a little askance. Generally people didn't specify who the drinks were for, but Carmel wanted to say the words. She collected the drinks and brought them down, sitting in the corner booth with them.

'Have you decided what you're going to do?' Luke asked as he lifted his pint to his mouth.

Carmel fought back the panic. She realised now that she was emotionally underdeveloped. She'd been reading a lot about children reared in care and how the normal human responses that happen between parents and kids and between kids and their siblings are often absent, and so it leads to emotional delay. Sometimes she felt like she was in a foreign world where everyone else spoke the language except her. Sharif understood

and wasn't put off by her odd reactions sometimes, but she hoped she could explain it properly
to the McDaids.

'I don't know. Jennifer and I spoke about it
briefly earlier. I'm a bit weird – that's the truth,
Luke. I've had such a peculiar life compared to
virtually everyone else I've met that I'm afraid to
move forward in case I mess it up. I don't really
understand about families, as I said, and what it's
OK to do and say. And I don't even know if I am
part of your family, so...' She sighed heavily,
knowing she was making a hash of explaining it
to him.

Luke waited to see if she would go on, and
when she didn't, he spoke. 'Will I tell you what I
think?'

She nodded at him.

'My dad thinks you are his child, and so if he's
sure, then that makes you my sister. And if you
want to be part of our family, then we'd love to
have you. When Dad first told me, I must admit I
was a bit like...I don't know, not shocked or anything, but just a bit slow to change things, y'-
know? Like, we're grand just the three of us. And
there was Mam as well, like, was it disloyal to her
or something? And let's face it – none of us like
to think of our parents as sexual beings, right?

189

And you being here meant that he did it with someone other than our mam, so that was a bit, I don't know, weird to process as well. But now that I've met you properly, and Sharif, as far as I'm concerned anyway, you're my sister and I think you should have the test.'

Carmel looked up into the intelligent green eyes of this man who might be her brother. 'And if I'm not?'

'Well, it won't matter to me. Or to Jennifer or to Dad, I'd say. I think the test will just confirm what we already know. You don't really look like him – but some of your mannerisms, and you have his laugh, that's the main reason I think so. It's inconceivable that you don't have McDaid blood in your veins, looking like you do. But even in the very unlikely event of it being negative, it will matter, of course, on one level, but it's not like we'd all just walk away and say, "OK, then, Carmel, nice knowing you."'

'But then I'm not your sister. My only point of connection with your family is someone I've never even met. The bond is so... Well, it's not there, is it? I think I don't want to do it because I'm afraid of what I'll find out. Wanting some-thing to be true and it actually being true are so different.' Carmel sipped her drink. The reality she couldn't say was that of course she was a Mc-Daid– but whose child was she?

'I love reading books about the law of attraction,' Carmel explained. 'Like, that our thoughts are things and that we can alter our lives by shaping our thoughts to what we want, *The Secret* and all of that. But then, when I was a little girl, all I wanted was a family. I prayed and wished and daydreamed all the time, but it never happened. And if the pure thoughts of a little child can't do it…'

Luke covered her hand with his and gave her a squeeze. He was just like his father, strong and protective, even though he was younger than her.

'I just mean that wishing for something and it actually happening are not the same thing.'

CHAPTER 20

'Relax.' Sharif put down his newspaper. 'It's going to be fine. You'll have a great day. It's going to be warm in central London, though, so don't forget your sun cream.'

'I know. And I don't know why I'm so nervous. It's like a date or something. That sounds stupid, I know, but I just… Oh, I don't know, Sharif.' Carmel leaned against the countertop with a cup of coffee in her hands.

'It's just a day out with someone you like and trust – what's to stress about? See the sights! I got Marlena to book front-row seats for *Jersey Boys* at the Odeon, and you have a reservation for pre-theatre dinner at the Five Fields in Chelsea –

have a few glasses of bubbly. Now, have you got your card? No scrimping now, OK? I know what you're like.' He stood and gathered his keys and wallet. 'Well, I'm seeing this new legal chap this morning, so I'd better get my skates on. I love you. Hopefully, if Luke can find out if this guy has a criminal record, then we can get a bit further with it. He rang me this morning, and based on the kind of behaviour Johnson has displayed to date, it wouldn't be strange that he's already well acquainted with law enforcement. He certainly looks the part. I called into Mrs Johnson yesterday and asked her about him, and the poor lady looked so nervous. She was lucid enough, but honestly, I think she's frightened of him. Just the mention of his name and she looked terrified.'

'He's awful.' Carmel shuddered. 'And he's been so rude and racist. I'm sure if there's anything to dig up, then Luke will do it. And as you say, he's just appeared out of nowhere. Nobody that ever knew her here even knew she had a son. It's all very suspicious.'

'Well,' Sharif said, 'it's helpful having someone like Luke to do some digging, that's for sure. Now I want you to forget about Julia and Bill and Derek Johnson and everything else and go off and have a great day with Joe.' He kissed her and was gone.

Joe was picking her up in twenty minutes, having seen Jennifer and the others to the airport, and then he and Carmel were taking the train together into London.

She'd had a lovely evening in the pub with Jennifer and Luke the night before, all stories and laughing, and she couldn't tell if she was so relaxed and happy around them because they really were her siblings or because she desperately wanted them to be. They didn't raise the subject of the DNA test again and just enjoyed each other's company. She observed Jennifer and Luke's interaction with a mixture of affection and envy. They were constantly teasing each other and had so many stories of the things they'd done together, not just as kids but as teenagers and young adults as well. They'd gone to Australia together to work for a year as part of a bigger group of friends and cousins; they'd backpacked around Thailand and Malaysia. They'd done so much and clearly were devoted to each other despite the banter. They were exactly what she imagined brothers and sisters to be like. Her only other experience was Bill and Julia, and the more time and distance she put between them, the more bizarre that set-up seemed to be. She told them stories of Bill, like the time he slept in the shed because he was nervous that the 'hippies', as he called them, were going to encircle the fairy tree that he was trying to cut down. Carmel had watched with well-concealed glee when the Friends of the Fairies, a bunch of weed-smoking vegans from England and Germany, decided that Bill was public enemy number one. They set up camps on the low fields, and Bill nearly went nuts. He got no backing from his neighbours either because everyone knew it was a disaster to cut down a fairy tree and terrible fortune awaited anyone associated with such endeavours. Bill wanted to drain the field, but the Friends of the Fairies refused him access and surrounded the tree. The local paper had got involved and everything. Luke and Jennifer were in stitches at her telling of it, and they could clearly just picture Bill sitting in wait in a cold shed, armed with a shotgun, waiting for the gang with their dreadlocks and hand-knit sweaters.

Her life in Ballyshanley had almost taken on caricature status as the time went on. She told them about the moving statue at the end of town that had drawn enormous crowds ten years ago, convinced the Virgin Mary was oscillating in some kind of Marian apparition. Ballyshanley shot to fame for about five minutes and had rapidly been devastated with disappointment when Ollie Kavanagh, the local electrician, changed the bulb illuminating the statue and she went back to being still once more. Ollie was not a popular person in town after that, mainly with Wheeler Cadogan, who'd invested in a huge mobile chip van to feed the faithful coming to see the moving statue, and his sister Delia, who had a thousand 'I saw the moving statue in Ballyshanley' t-shirts printed thinking she'd make a killing.

Carmel had never thought of herself as remotely amusing, though the nuns did chuckle at her sometimes, but everyone seemed to think she was very funny these days. It was nice to be able to make people laugh, she found.

She checked her wallet for cash. It never ceased to give her a thrill that she had money of her own. Bill used to give the girls wads of cash when they visited, and Carmel would look in amazement at his largesse when she had virtually no money. The local grocery shop was on an account, which he settled each month, and everything else was paid for by the month, so it never occurred to him that she might like to have some money. Once she saw an ad up in the local shop for a housekeeper job in the town and mentioned to him that she might apply. He'd looked at her as if she were stark staring mad.

'Skivvying for the neighbours – would you have sense?' was all he said, then wearily went back to his farm, leaving Carmel with the all-too-familiar sensation of having let him down once again.

It wasn't that she wanted to buy anything in particular, but it just would have been nice to have her own money, to be able to pop into the Cosy Corner Café for tea and a scone or to buy herself a book or a new top or whatever.

Bill had an account in Cotter's, the local draper's shop, where he bought three shirts every year as well as six new vests and six new pairs of underpants and pyjamas. Every five years, he bought a suit. The girls and Carmel usually got him a pullover and socks for Christmas, and Julia bought him slippers. The suits had three phases: the Good Suit, the newest, used for Mass, weddings and funerals; the Five-Year-Old Suit, used for going to the mart, for a pint or to the occasional football match or hare coursing event; and the Ten-Year-Old Suit, used for farming. They were all identical, dark brown and made of a kind of hairy material that only seemed to ever be used in old men's suits in rural Ireland. They just got baggier and shinier with age.

Up to the time Carmel left, she was turning the collars on his shirts to get extra wear out of them. Sharif had been incredulous at that and said it reminded him of stories people told him about living with rationing and deprivations during the war. He had no idea that anyone was still displaying such unnecessary frugality.

Once Carmel saw overalls on special offer in the draper's, so she bought them for Bill, thinking they would be better than the suit, but he told her to take them back, that they were a waste of money. The draper's had some women's clothes as well, and Carmel did get a few things there, but the owner, Mrs Cotter, was a lady in her seventies, as tall as she was wide, and her taste in stock reflected that. Pastel cardigans, pleated skirts, lilac or pink blouses, support stockings and gigantic interlock knickers seemed to be the only things she had for sale. Carmel had taken to secreting a little of the 'housekeeping' money for her own things. Bill put twenty euros a week in a jar for sundries in case they ran out, and she siphoned off a few euros each week. Over months, she managed to save up enough to buy an occasional pair of jeans or a top – suitable for someone under the age of seventy – in the charity shop or sometimes the large department store at the edge of town.

CHAPTER 21

*C*armel remembered the day Julia had caught her coming out of the St Vincent de Paul shop. Julia had nearly had a fit and berated Carmel at length that evening, saying that the whole place would be talking about the fact that she, the wife of one of the strongest farmers in the locality, was in the charity shop. Julia insisted that if anyone asked, Carmel was to say she was making a donation, not buying anything. Even though Bill was there – although he was reading the paper – during this verbal bashing, it never occurred to either him or Julia to ask how Carmel bought clothes or anything for herself.

Every birthday, the girls bought her a scarf, usually some shade of blue – she had seventeen of them by the time she left – and Julia bought her slippers too, usually brown or navy tartan. She thought of the lovely pink fluffy ones she'd bought with her first week's wages. Bill just gave her the voucher for the electrical shop – it was an excruciatingly formal and embarrassing exchange each year – and she managed to make it stretch to buy phone credit and a few small personal items. Her life in Bedfordshire was the opposite; she had a wardrobe full of lovely clothes and a drawer containing silk lingerie, and on the fitted shoe rack, there were eight pairs of shoes. It seemed almost criminal decadence.

The knock on the door startled her out of her reverie. She took one quick glance in the mirror and decided she looked OK. She was wearing trainers because there was going to be a lot of walking, light blue jeans and a cream hoodie. Her blonde hair was tied up in a ponytail, and she wondered if she was a bit old for such a girly look; she was going to take it down when Joe knocked again. Dismissing her hair concerns, she opened the door.

Joe smiled and enveloped her in a hug.

'Coffee?' she asked, hoping her voice didn't betray her nerves. It was ridiculous; it wasn't as if she had never met him. But this day, this time alone together, was a first, and she felt so unsure.

'Please, if you're making some anyway.'

'I've it made already.'

'God, Carmel, I...I might as well tell you, I was so nervous coming over here. I was trying to give myself a good talking to. Like, I know you and everything now, but I don't know...'

'Me too. I feel exactly the same.'

'It's like a first date, isn't it?' He chuckled.

'Well, since I've never had that experience, I don't know. I never went on a date with Bill, and Sharif just sort of showed up and we were together and that was that. No dating as such... though I'm not complaining, mind you. I don't know what I'd say or do on a proper date with a stranger.' Carmel felt she was babbling, but it seemed to relax them both.

'Well, whatever way you got together, it sounds to me like a great day's work. He's a lovely man and he's mad about you – anyone can see that. I'm so glad he rescued you from that desperate situation. You deserve to be happy after all you've been through. I just wish you didn't have to...' Joe seemed visibly upset, thinking about Carmel's life up to the time Sharif appeared.

'It wasn't that bad, honestly,' she tried to reassure him.

'You say that, but I hate the thought of you as a little girl in that home on the North Circular Road. God knows how many times I passed it over the years. I remember when Mary used to get the bus home sometimes, she'd sit upstairs for the view of the city, and she'd often remark at what a cheerless-looking place that was. I'm ashamed to say I never thought too much about it, but now that I've discovered you spent your childhood there, I feel like I should have stormed the place.'

Carmel giggled. 'Well, you wouldn't get far, let me tell you. Sister Kevin and Sister Margaret were some operators, and one man wouldn't faze them a bit.' Carmel saw his face was so sad when he thought about her childhood and wanted to reassure him as she did Sharif. 'They were kind, Joe, honestly they were. And the other kids were nice and we had good times. It might have looked dreary or whatever, but we didn't know what we were missing, you know? And it really was grand.'

He shrugged. 'Maybe so, but then the thought of you being stuck out in the sticks with that thick farmer, when all the time you could have been in a happy family, adopted by people who'd love you properly, all because of my father...' Joe wiped his eye, brushing away a tear. 'I'm sorry, Carmel. I'm a big eejit, dragging all that back up again when you probably want to forget it, but it just sickens me when I think about it.'

Carmel handed Joe his coffee. 'Look, Joe, it wasn't great, OK? Nobody's saying it was. But it wasn't that bad either. I keep telling people that, but they don't want to believe it. I was fed and clothed and educated, and honestly, it was fine. And the years with Bill, well, it wasn't like he was cruel or hurt me or anything. It was just, well, more of the same really, I suppose.'

'But we all need love, Carmel.' He sounded so sincere.

'Maybe,' she conceded. 'And a life where you're loved is – well, I can't explain just how different it is, but I never knew what that felt like anyway, so I never knew what I was missing. I thought families were always fighting and people cheated on each other all the time, either that or they lived in totally unrealistic situations. All my education about real life came from TV and watching the soaps, you see.'

CHAPTER 22

*J*oe leaned against the kitchen counter, cupping his coffee with both hands. 'Just because you knew no better doesn't make what he did acceptable. I hated my father long before I knew about you, really hated him, and the day he died was a great day. God knows we waited long enough. He was a bully and a liar, and he made our lives and my mother's life hell. What saved us was each other. Myself, Colm, Brian, Kevin and the girls, we looked out for each other and for Mam too. Brian told you about the time I battered him, put him in the hospital because I came in to find him hitting my ma and I just saw red. What he didn't tell you was it was Brian that pulled me off him. I'd have killed him, Carmel. I find that hard to say. I'm not a violent man, never raised my fists in anger at anyone before or since, but something about him, the smug, holier-than-thou way he went on. He'd make you sick, so he would, up there on the altar at Mass, doing the readings and giving out communion, looking like butter wouldn't melt, when all the time, he was anything but. I pressured my ma to go to the Guards and press charges, but she wouldn't. It was peculiar back then. Like, the woman was somehow shamed as well if her husband was beating her, or maybe she was just afraid of him. Anyway, she wouldn't make a statement to the Guards. I made sure that people knew, though, me and Dolly. I was over at her house after the fight happened – I couldn't go home – and I remember my hands were all swollen and I had all of these cuts on my knuckles. She patched me up. I was giving out that my ma wouldn't go to the Guards, and says she, "Listen, Joe, if the reason you want her to go and report him is so that his reputation as a pillar of the community is shattered by having to turn up to face charges in court, well, we can't make sure he goes to court but we can make sure everyone knows what he really is. That's easily done. Just tell Bina O'Leary. She's got the biggest gob in the parish, and just watch the story take on legs and arms and all sorts. People love something to gossip about. They half know anyway. Sure we've all seen your ma with so many injuries, and people aren't thick. So we tell Bina and we'll leave it to her to fill in the juicy details – she'd love nothing more. Don't you worry – they'll be giving each other knowing glances and secret sneers by next Sunday if he's out of hospital in time for Mass.'"

Joe chuckled. 'Of course she was right. Bina ran the small shop at the end of our road and prided herself on knowing everyone's business. Dolly went up to buy some disinfectant, even though we had loads, and told Bina the whole story, all upset like, about him and my ma, and me attacking him and the whole lot. And sure enough, the whole place had it by the next day. Not just that he was battering my mother, but the girls as well, and that he'd been cautioned by the Guards, and that he was facing prison if he did it again – oh, Bina went the whole nine yards. My mam was upset at the start, but she didn't know how it got out. She never did. And you know, people were kind, not as judgemental as she thought they might be, and in a way, it protected her. Now that it was out what kind of a man he was, she couldn't be going around saying she walked into the door or whatever, so he had to lay off a bit.' The look on his face said his father didn't stop completely, however.

'Go on,' Carmel urged. This was her family history now, no matter how hard to hear.

Joe continued. 'When he got out of hospital, he went into the church to make sure nobody had usurped him in his position of chief arse-licker. He was always monsignor this and the reverend that, making out like himself and the bishop were best mates. The big eejit. Anyway the parish priest was Father O'Mahony, a big gruff fella from Connemara, hands like shovels and no patience for hypocrites like him. He gave him the road apparently, saying he'd want to mend his ways and repent of his sins before darkening the door of his church again. And he did it in front of the women cleaning and doing the flowers for the altar, so it gave more fuel to the fire started by Bina. The priest knew what he was like, because my ma had gone to him once or twice when we were kids, looking for help. He used to give her a few bob, or get a box of grub sent around. He was a grand man really, and I'd say my father's carry on, being all holy for show and a tyrant at home, appalled him. My father was finished then. His reputation was all he had and that was in tatters, but he was more dangerous now in some ways because he was so bitter.' Joe placed his cup in the sink, rinsing it and putting it in to drain. He had to compose himself.

'What he did to Dolly...my lovely Dolly... She was brave as a lion, Carmel, she really was. Nothing scared her, and she was so loyal. That's why, when she left without a word, I was devastated. Not just for a while either, but for years. It was so unlike her. I could never accept that she just walked away from everyone, from me. She wasn't that kind of person. My wife, Mary, knew all about it, everyone did, as I looked such a misery for so long after. Mary and I didn't mention it much, she questioned me before we married and then we left it after that, but when she was dying, we did. She said she thought I never really got over Dolly leaving, and she was right. But knowing why she had to go, well, it's so hard to come to terms with.' He sighed heavily. 'Would you listen to me, dragging all this up on a sunny morning when we are supposed to be going for a nice day out. I'm sorry, Carmel.'

'Don't be. It's our shared history, and it's good that we can talk about it. Dolly carried that secret, and then Brian did, and now it's ours to carry, but at least we have each other.'

Joe looked deeply into her eyes, neither of them speaking for a moment. 'I'm a simple man, Carmel. I've gone over this and over it since Brian's funeral, and I just keep coming to the same conclusion. As far as I'm concerned, you're my daughter, and though I don't know you well yet, I love you and want the best for you just as I do for my other two kids. I'm happy to go to my grave with things just as they are. So it's up to you. If you want to do the test, or if you never do, then that's OK and we can forget all about tests and DNA and all of that. But I have to ask you this.' He took a steadying breath. 'Do you want me to be your dad? Because if you don't, then just say so. I keep thinking this must feel like a runaway train. Maybe you had no notion of involving yourself with us but it was me who barged in on you demanding answers, so if you want out now, then that's OK.'

It was as if a dam were released within her. Carmel couldn't stop it. All the years, all the rejection, just seemed to take on a molten quality and fell as scalding-hot tears. She tried to speak, but no words would come. She was five again, seven, twelve, twenty-one, a bride, lonely.

Joe just stood right in front of her, not touching, not speaking. The tears racked her body, and she found it hard to breathe. She had no idea where all of this was coming from, and it frightened her. She gulped air, tried to steady her breath, but she couldn't. She was so overwhelmed by her reaction that she couldn't even feel embarrassed at her lack of control.

Pain seared Joe's face, seeing her in such anguish, and eventually he stretched out his arms. He made no move towards her, but his arms were welcoming her. If she moved into his embrace now, then that would be it. She wanted to, but she was afraid. She desperately wanted him to be her father, to love and protect her. Even though she was forty-one years old, she felt like she was a child. Suddenly something propelled her forward. She didn't know what it was, but she had the same feeling she'd had that night outside the pub in Dublin when Sharif asked her to come back to London with him. They had been singing her mother's song, 'Que Sera, Sera,' at a party in the pub, and Carmel felt Dolly urging her to trust Sharif. She felt her again now.

She took the two steps towards him and felt his arms around her. She sobbed into his shirt, and he rubbed her back and kissed the top of her head, soothing her gently.

'I do want you to be my dad,' she managed to croak.

'Well, then' – Joe smiled through his own tears, his strong arms tightening around her – 'I am. It's OK, darling. You're home now. It's all right. I've got you. Nothing will ever hurt you. I've got you, my lovely baby girl. You're safe.' He murmured those words over and over again, and she eventually felt herself relax and her breathing return to normal. The front of his shirt was soaked, and she could hear his heart beating through his chest. He smelled of washing powder and aftershave. She felt so safe. They stood together for a long time, the sun streaming in the window, locked in their own little space in the world together. Eventually, he released her and they smiled at each other.

'Thanks.' She wiped her face with a tissue he offered her. 'I'm sorry about that. I don't know what happened there, just years of...I don't know.'

'Anytime, pet. I've a lot of making up to do.'

CHAPTER 23

They had a fantastic day walking all over London. Joe took her to see where he lived with his Bangladeshi friend off the Tottenham Court Road years ago, and she showed him some of the places Sharif had shared with her. They held hands on the London Eye and shared their meals at the fantastic restaurant Sharif had booked for them, realising they both were mushroom lovers but were very dubious about cheese. Sharif sent her a few texts during the day, just checking in with her, and she assured him that she was having a wonderful time. They sang along to all the songs in *Jersey Boys*, and after the show went for a drink in a cosy old pub.

They were so engrossed in each other's company, it was as if the rest of the world didn't exist. He told her all about his years working his own butcher shop, and how he'd been able to take early retirement because he'd bought a few houses in Dublin when they were cheap and had done them up himself; he loved carpentry and wiring and plumbing. Now he could live on the rental income on top of his pension. He told her about the apartment he'd bought outside Malaga in Spain and how it was for anyone in the family who wanted to use it. She told him that she'd never been anywhere but England before the week in France with Sharif and that she'd love to go to Spain with him sometime. They were lost in conversation about tapas and sangria when they were interrupted.

'Excuse me, do you mind if we sit here?' An elderly couple had approached, and the man indicated the other end of their table. The woman was dressed in the kind of outfit sold by Mrs Cronin in Ballyshanley, a neat mauve cardigan and skirt and a primrose-yellow blouse underneath. She had the impossible kind of tight curls worn by ladies of a certain age, and Carmel knew instinctively a lot of energy had gone into the woman's big night out. She had a lined, careworn face, but there was kindness there too.

'Of course, no problem.' Joe smiled and moved up a little.

While the man went to the bar, the woman sat down and began to chat. 'We've just been to see *Jersey Boys* – our son bought us tickets for our anniversary. We don't normally come into the West End – we're from Croydon – but it's very nice, isn't it?'

Carmel really just wanted Joe all to herself, but the woman seemed like a nice old lady. Carmel did hope, though, that once her husband came back, they'd be left alone again. 'Yes, we've just seen it too. We really enjoyed it.'

'Really? Isn't that funny? Well, I suppose it is just across the road, so maybe not that much of a coincidence. My Ernie is always saying I'm seeing signs where there's nothing. Maybe he's right. Very superstitious, I am. Can't help it – always have been since I was a little 'un. One night, during the Blitz, we were worn out from going down the Tube station night after night. My dad said he was sleeping in his own bed and if Hitler wanted to come, then let him. So we all stayed in the house, delighted to be sleeping in a bed and not all squashed up together in the smelly old Tube. But something woke me up, and I went into my parents' room. I was only five or six. I told them to get up, the Germans were coming. Of course they told me to go back to bed, that there hadn't even been a siren, but I insisted. Eventually my mum said there was something about me, so she bundled us all up and took us back down the Elephant and Castle station again, dragging my poor old dad grumbling behind her. Next morning, though, our house was gone, flattened in a direct hit. Anyway, listen to me, blathering on. So is it a special occasion for you too, anniversary or something?'

Joe grinned at the idea that he and Carmel were a couple.

'No...well, yes, actually.' Carmel thrilled at what she was about to say. 'Joe here is my dad, and we've only just been reunited. I never knew him growing up, but he's back in my life now.'

'Well, isn't that just smashing!' The woman couldn't have looked more pleased if she'd been told she'd won the lottery. 'I love that show, *Long Lost Family*, you know, the one with Davina Mc-Call and that other chap, where they find people all over the world? It's amazing. And then people are so happy to see each other again. Blood is thicker than water – isn't that the truth? Sometimes it doesn't work out, of course, but looking at you two, you're going to be fine, I'd say.' She spoke to Joe directly. 'She's like you.' Then she turned to Carmel. 'But your mum must be a looker too.'

'She's dead unfortunately, but she was lovely,' Carmel said, worried Joe would be too choked up.

'Oh, I am sorry, but you know what? I bet she's here now, watching over you both, delighted to see you two together after all these years. Don't force it, would be my advice. Que sera, sera, as the old song goes – do you know it? Doris Day.' She began to sing softly. 'Que sera, sera... Whatever will be, will be...The future's not ours to see...'

At that moment, Ernie came back, nodded politely at them and led his wife to a table that had just become vacant at the other end of the bar.

Joe and Carmel smiled incredulously. She'd shown him the video of Dolly singing that song at her birthday party, and he told her that it was her party piece, even as a kid. Then she told him about how they were singing it in the pub that first night she met Sharif. And now this.

They sat together in the back of the cab all the way home, Carmel nestled against him, his arm around her shoulder. He told her stories of his childhood, his mother and his siblings, and they talked a lot about Dolly. Carmel felt the picture of her mother was becoming clearer every minute.

Sharif and Nadia had told her so much about her mother's life in London, and now Joe was able to fill in all about her life in Ireland. Carmel's maternal grandfather had been dead many years, and according to Joe, he was heartbroken when Dolly left without a word. Joe had plagued him for months, convinced he knew where she was, but eventually he'd had to give up when Austin Mullane broke down, something nobody had ever seen, and roared at Joe to leave him alone. It was bad enough that he'd lost his wife and then his only child without the neighbours mithering him day and night about it.

'He was a nice man, Carmel, your granddad, easy-going, quiet. I don't really remember Dolly's mother – she was dead very young. TB, I think. Back then in the '50s it was rampant. Austin was of his generation, not great with the feelings and all of that, but Dolly was his whole world. Some-times I'd see him watching her and she trick-acting around him, and his face glowed with love and pride. He'd never say it, even to her, but she meant the world to him.'

'Maybe we could go to see his grave sometime if I come back to Dublin?' Carmel wanted to connect, even if it was to lay some flowers on his grave.

'Of course we will, pet, and I'll take you to Nana Mac's as well – that's what all the grandkids called my ma. She was lovely. It will be some party when we tell the extended McDaids about you! Well, you met some of them at Brian's funeral, so you know what they're like, so imagine that multiplied by about fifty. Actually, my niece Aisling – she's Colm's daughter – is getting married in a few months. I'm sure she'd love you to come. Jennifer and Damien and Luke, of course, will be there too. Would you and Sharif come?'

'If she wouldn't mind, then we'd love to.'

'Nah, she'll be delighted. Aisling's gas. Did you meet her at the funeral?'

'I did. She seemed lovely.'

'Speaking of the funeral, I was wondering if I should make contact with Brian's friend, the landlord man who came to the funeral? Do you know him? What do you think?'

Carmel had discussed this with Sharif, and they had concluded that if Joe brought it up, then the best thing would be to tell him the truth. Tim was feeling very alone, but he was never going to reach out to the McDaids after all this time. Knowing what she knew about the family now, Carmel felt sure they would welcome him too, and perhaps his life need not be so lonely.

'Tim, yes. I've got to know him since Brian was admitted. Dolly told Tim to bring him when it got too much. I see him now from time to time. He's heartbroken, really he is.'

'Well, if he and Brian were such good friends, I'd like to meet him again, but I don't know – English people are different to us. Do you think he'd see it as an intrusion?'

Carmel sat up and turned to face him. 'No, I don't. The first thing is, he's not English. He's from County Mayo, though he's lived here for years...'

Joe sensed her hesitation. 'And the second thing?'

'Well, the second thing is...' – she hoped her revelation wasn't going to shock Joe or make him think less of his brother – 'he and Brian weren't just friends. Brian was gay, and he and Tim were together for over forty years.'

'You're joking.' Joe was astounded. 'Seriously? I can't believe that. Like, we had no idea...'

'Are you shocked?'

'No.' Joe shook his head and smiled. 'Not like

shocked horrified or anything. I'm a bit sad, I suppose, that he felt he couldn't tell us, tell me even. I thought we were closer than that... I thought he felt he could trust me.'

Carmel hated to hear the hurt in Joe's voice. 'He absolutely did trust you,' she said with certainty. 'And when Brian and I spoke about everything, he told me how close you two were, how much he felt for you when Dolly left and how hard he went on her to allow him to tell you the truth. He cared about you so much, genuinely, but I think he just wanted to keep his private life private. To be honest, I got the impression it was more for Tim's sake – he was married for years and years and had kids and everything. Apart from the fact that for many years it was illegal. I think the reason he never told you was because Tim was afraid his kids would get wind of it. Tim still sees them, and they have no idea – they think Brian was a lodger. Apparently, he had his own room, and anyone walking into the house would never think anything other than that two bachelors were sharing a house. It's not as strange over here as it might be at home. Property is so expensive here, loads of people share.'

Joe digested this information and made a decision. 'Right, OK. Well, in that case, I definitely want to go and see him. Will you come with me? It would be easier, I think, if you were there.'

'Of course I will. You're stuck with me now... Dad.' It was the first time she'd ever called him that, and though she couldn't see his face as she nestled back into him in the darkness of the cab, she knew he was smiling.

CHAPTER 24

*C*armel crawled quietly into bed beside Sharif, who was fast asleep. He instantly woke with the movement.

'I'm sorry. I was trying not to wake you,' Carmel whispered.

Sharif turned and gathered her into his arms. 'I was only dozing. I knew you were on the way – thanks for the text. You know I didn't mind if you wanted to stay out, but it's nice to know you're OK. Did you have fun?'

'Oh, Sharif, we had the best time, but I'll tell you all about it tomorrow. Go back to sleep.'

'No, it's OK. I've been resting all evening. Tell me everything. How was the show?'

'Amazing. We were singing along and everything. The strange thing is, on the way there, we were trying to think of Frankie Valli songs we might know and came up with around two, and then we knew every single one. It was such fun. And then we met this lady in the bar who actually sang a bit of "Que Sera, Sera", I mean, those exact words. I know some people might think that's a load of old rubbish, but I don't – I think it was Dolly telling us that she was happy Joe and I were reunited.'

'And did you talk about that, the test and everything?'

She told him everything, all about the breakdown in the apartment before they left and about the test and Tim and everything they'd discussed.

'I'm glad you told him. I could never have said anything, confidentiality and so on, but Tim told you and therefore you could tell Joe, and I think it will be nice for them to meet properly. It must have been so hard for Tim, being the person Brian was closest to and having to behave like they were something less than that. Joe is such a nice man. I'm sure he'll welcome Tim to the Mc-Daid family, just as he's welcomed you.'

'He really is special, you know. The more I get to know him, the more I think Joe's just like the fathers I imagined as a kid, strong, kind, funny, that sort of thing. I was sitting in the back of the taxi, and he had his arm around me, and I was cuddled up to him. I just didn't feel forty-one – I felt about ten – and he made me feel safe. It's scary for me. I'm not used to all this affection, either from you or from him, and yet it all feels natural, right somehow. I just keep thinking this can't actually be happening to me.'

'So are you going to see Tim with him?'

'Yes, tomorrow afternoon if possible. Joe is going to call him in the morning and see if he's free. I think he's kind of nervous about it. He was sad that Brian never told him, and he seemed genuinely surprised.'

'I suppose Brian wasn't in the least bit camp or anything, not that all gay men are, but he didn't conform to any of the stereotypes of gay people we see on TV or whatever. He was very strait-laced, I suppose, and even when Tim visited, if anything, they seemed kind of formal with each other.'

'I suppose when you have to live your real life in secret, you build up walls like that. It's hard to imagine it now, I mean, looking at people like Zane, who are out and proud and happy, no matter what his father thinks, but that's relatively new.' Carmel sighed. 'Poor Brian. It must have been so hard to go home and pretend he was single.'

'Well, he at least had the guts to get up and live the life he wanted to live, unlike many of his compatriots. It's the same in my culture, worse actually, as homosexuality is still technically illegal in Pakistan, and even if the law isn't enforced that much, there's still a terrible stigma. Britain has proved to be such a sanctuary for so many gay people from our part of the world. If Pakistanis didn't have British passports because of being in the Commonwealth, well, I dread to think. It gave people an out, someplace to go, and getting here was like the Holy Grail. My dad used to tell me the lengths people would go to, to get enough money to emigrate to Britain, and once they managed it, they loved this country with a devotion they had never displayed for their homeland.'

'You wouldn't want to let a bunch of Irish nuns hear you say that.' Carmel chuckled. 'We were fed a strict diet of the trials and misery brought down on our heads because of the English for 800 years. They'd go mental if they heard someone saying being ruled by Britain was actually a good thing.' Carmel leaned on one elbow and looked down into Sharif's face.

'I don't think any Irish nuns would approve of a good Irish Catholic girl consorting with a Pakistani lapsed Muslim either.' He smiled ruefully. 'Especially one facing a malpractice suit.'

'Tell me if you don't want to talk about it, but how was your day? Meeting the other solicitor, how did that go?'

He sighed deeply, and she saw the worry cross his face once more. 'All right, I suppose. It seems that all he has are these photos, which are definitely fake. The sheets are not ones we use – they have patterns on them, and everything we use here is white – so he obviously put the stains on them, brought them in and put them on his mother's bed and photographed her. The dirty tray, the ashtray, I've never seen any of it before. But the solicitor said the same as my own legal people, that it would be best to settle. Luke rang. Apparently this Johnson does have a record, but it's all for petty things, so nothing we could really use. The solicitor reckons that scumbag's not even going to try to take it into court, but that he might just try to blackmail me, say he'll send the photos to the papers or something, or post them online. Who knows? He's sent a letter – I got a copy this morning – outlining all his grievances. Not just the dirt and all of that, but that people here are cruel to his mother, that she doesn't get her meds on time, that she's just not being taken care of generally. His legal representative is not one my solicitor had ever heard of, but that doesn't mean anything.'

'This is just so wrong!' Carmel struggled to control her temper. 'How the hell can he just come up with all this stuff? And poor Mrs Johnson can't even speak up for us. We've done nothing but be kind and courteous and look after her, like we do for everyone, and this awful money-grabbing man can just... I've a good mind to find him and...'

'I know. It's infuriating. Trust me, I was stomping around the office when I got the letter, so I went for a run. Pounding the roads seemed to work the temper out of me. I know the temptation, darling, to find him and force him to withdraw his ridiculous claims. Believe me, I have fantasised about this myself. But we must do nothing that would make us in any way culpable. All the legal people agree on that. Do not approach him and keep an extra-close eye on Mrs Johnson, keep her charts, her paperwork all up to date and verified. I am having another consultant come in tomorrow to assess her and write a report on her care, just to have it. I've asked Tristan to recommend someone, not anybody I know, to have an independent assessment of her for our files. It's going to be a rocky road ahead, Carmel, and I can't tell you how glad I am to have you beside me.'

'Well, I've a confession to make. I actually did approach him the other day in the car park. I thought I might be able to get through to him, or try to figure out what was wrong with him at least. He basically told me that we, the Paddy and the Paki, should both go back where we came from and stop scrounging off the British state.'

Sharif laughed out loud. 'Says the only one in this whole sorry story on state benefits! He really is a piece of work. Was that all? I hope he didn't hurt you?'

'No, just verbally abusive and racist. What you'd expect. He is so smelly and horrible, and his car – ugh, gross.'

'I know. Look, it will hopefully be OK, and you know how I know that?' He put his arms around her.

'No, how?'

'Because I have you in my corner. I'd be so much more worried if I were facing this alone. But having you beside me, well, it's just great.'

'Always. I don't know how much help I can be, but I'm here one hundred percent.'

'I know you are. Now we had better get some sleep – busy day tomorrow.' His dark eyes fixed on hers. 'Unless you're not sleepy?' A slow smile crossed his handsome face.

Feeling quite wanton, as the nuns might have put it, she ran her hand over his chest. 'No, I think I could stay awake if I were busy…'

CHAPTER 25

*C*armel's beeper buzzed her to reception. She tried not to show her frustration at being called away.

She really wanted to finish her paperwork and have everything all sorted before meeting Joe. He had arranged to call to Tim's house at six and was picking her up at five thirty. She took out her phone again. She'd read the text several times already, but she couldn't stop herself.

How's my girl this morning? Really had a fantastic day yesterday, pet, one of the best of my life. Meeting Tim at his house at 6. Will I pick you up at 5:30? Love, Dad xx

She'd offered to meet him earlier, but he said

he had a few things to do before flying back to Ireland the following morning so he'd see her later. She wondered what he could have to do in London. While she wanted to spend as much time as she could with him, she was glad to get to pitch in with the musical. She had to keep reminding herself that Joe and his family were in her life now and that there would be many more chances for them to meet.

As she made her way to reception, her phone beeped again. Another text, this time from a number she didn't know.

Hi, Carmel. I'm Aisling. Uncle Joe said he'd like for you to come to my wedding, so if you and Sharif are free on the 15th of March, I'd love to see you again. We met at Uncle Brian's funeral, but I'm looking forward to meeting you properly, now that we know who you are! Hope you can come, Aisling xx

Carmel was so touched by the message, as well as that Joe had asked Aisling to invite her in the first place, and then that Aisling had taken the trouble to contact Carmel herself. Every moment since making the decision not to have the test had made her realise what a good choice it was. She felt like Joe's daughter, she wanted to be part of his family, and finding out for sure might jeopardise all of that, so she was glad. To go from having nobody at all to having not just Sharif and Nadia but now being part of this big, noisy family…well, it was a dream come true.

She would wait till later to reply to Aisling when she could word it properly, something to convey how grateful she was for their acceptance.

Joe was standing in reception.

'Is everything OK?' She rushed over to him; he looked a little shaken. 'I thought we weren't meeting until later?'

'Yes, don't worry, everything is grand. I just needed to see you. I need to talk to you, you and Sharif actually, urgently. Is he around?'

Carmel could tell from his expression that something had definitely happened. All sorts ran through her head. Maybe he had decided against taking on Dolly's daughter; maybe someone in his family had talked sense into him.

'Em…yes, I can have him beeped. Let's go in here.' She led him into an office off the large sunny reception area. Before entering, she turned to Marlena. 'Marlena, can you beep Sharif, please? Tell him it's urgent. Thanks.'

She closed the door and they both stood in silence. Whatever had happened, Carmel knew it was not good. Joe looked stern and preoccupied. 'Can I get you a drink? Tea? Coffee?' It sounded so ridiculously formal after the intimacy of the day before.

'No, pet, nothing. I'm fine.'

At least he called her 'pet'. That was a sign he still loved her, wasn't it? Or maybe he used that term of endearment with lots of people and it didn't mean anything special with her. He stood with his back to the room, gazing out the window.

'Joe, Sharif is on the way, but please, can you tell me what's wrong? Did I do something wrong?'

He turned. 'You? You do something wrong? Ah, Carmel, my love, you're completely innocent, but somebody's doing something wrong all right...'

Sharif opened the door. 'What is it? Are you OK, Carmel?' Worry was etched on his face. She'd never had him beeped before. She would normally just text him, but he sometimes didn't read messages if he was with a patient. The beep was really just for emergencies.

Before she had time to answer, Joe spoke. 'Sit down, both of you. You're going to want to hear this.'

Carmel and Sharif exchanged a glance, neither having a clue what was coming next. They sat on one of the sofas Sharif provided for the many difficult conversations he had to have in that room, usually delivering news on the health of a loved one. He had a desk and a chair in there too, but usually he sat with the families, opposite them on the other sofa. Sharif reached for Carmel's hand.

'So, Carmel,' Joe began, his jaw set in a determined line, 'this morning I went to see a solicitor here in town. I had to sort out some things regarding Brian's estate. He had some investments in Ireland, but he left all his paperwork in perfect order so I knew where to go. I also thought I could kill two birds, as it were, and make my own will. I know I could have done it at home as well, but I wanted to have something to show you this evening, just so you'd know I was serious when I said I want you in my family. Luke and Jennifer are always onto me about doing it, and so I decided I was going to split my estate three ways, equally between my three children, you, Jennifer and Luke.'

Carmel had no idea what to say; such a huge gesture was really overwhelming. Before she had time to process it, however, Joe went on.

'So I went into Bedford this morning – that's

where Brian's solicitor is based, at Old Weir Legal Centre. It's only a mile or two from here, actually. There I was, anyway, waiting in the sort of communal area. It's like a chambers for loads of legal people – you know the place?'

Sharif nodded. 'I do.'

'Well, anyway, I was a bit early, so I was just waiting when two people came in. He was fifty-ish, unkempt looking, tattoos and all that, and he was with a woman, similar age. The first thing I noticed was she had an Irish accent, and then I looked again. They walked past me and sat kind of around the corner, and though they were talking quietly and didn't imagine they could be overheard, I got most of the conversation. The woman was clearly in charge and was telling the man what to say to the solicitor. Apparently, they were meeting someone new, since their old solicitor appeared to have abandoned them and their case.'

Carmel had no idea where this was going but felt her stomach lurch.

Joe went on. 'She was telling him not to play up anything too much apart from the photos, that that was their downfall the last time, that all of that was going to be contested by staff but that the camera didn't lie. Lads, she was talking about here and Mrs Johnson.'

Sharif shook his head, astounded. 'I got a call from my legal people this morning, saying that they didn't know why, but Johnson's old solicitor just rang to say he wasn't dealing with the case any more. He wouldn't go any further, apparently, just that.'

'Exactly. Well, according to this pair, the old solicitor was hopeless and didn't want to bend the rules, so their mission was to engage another one. That's what they were doing at the law firm.'

'Describe the woman.' Carmel's voice was monotone. She had a horrible feeling she knew who it was.

'Very thin, darkish hair drawn back from her face. I didn't get a good look at her, because, as I said, they were around the corner. He never referred to her by name, but she was definitely running the show. He's English, a bit of a half-wit, at least that's how he came across.'

'It's Julia.' Carmel was shocked but certain. 'I'd put my life on it. This whole thing is her doing. She said back in Ireland that I would pay for what I did to her, and again the other day, and so she's using this Johnson eejit to get back at us, get back at me, really, for daring to try to divorce Bill and break up the farm.'

The silence hung heavily in the room as they processed what Carmel had just said.

Eventually Joe spoke again. 'I think you're right. He kept going on about how much they should settle for, trying to calculate Sharif's worth. I was called in then. I didn't want to go, but if I didn't, it would have looked suspicious, and I didn't want them to know they'd been overheard. I made my excuses to the solicitor. I think she thought I was just too upset over Brian, so she was very kind and told me there was no rush and to call back when I'm ready. I came straight here.'

They sat in silence for a moment.

'Did you actually hear them say it was a fake photo?' Sharif asked.

'No, no, I didn't, just that he was to leave the talking to her and to stick to the photos, that nothing else was provable.'

Carmel could tell Joe was disappointed that he hadn't more conclusive proof that Julia and Johnson were in cahoots.

'So what should we do now? Surely this shows they're telling lies?' Carmel felt sure it must mean something.

'I don't know. I'm totally out of my depth here. Should we go to the police?' Sharif wondered.

'Maybe we should ask Luke,' Joe suggested. 'Like, I know it's policing in a different jurisdiction, but he might know what to do?'

CHAPTER 26

'Can't hurt.' Sharif thought for a moment. 'But we're going to have to be very clever about this. This might be a breakthrough, but it's still only your word against theirs, and you are Carmel's father, so you'd be bound to defend her. You said there was nobody else there?'

'Not a soul unfortunately.' Joe's brow furrowed in frustration. 'So will I ring Luke now? See what he says?'

'Please do. Thanks, Joe,' Sharif replied, deep in thought as Joe went over to the other end of the room to contact his son.

Carmel felt such guilt, she had to say something. 'Sharif, I'm so, so sorry. This is all my fault, bringing that evil witch into your life... I just –'

'Stop,' he whispered, clearly trying not to disturb Joe as he tried to make contact with Luke. He cupped her face in his hands and spoke directly to her. 'None of this is your fault, or mine, not anyone else's but Derek Johnson's and possibly your ex-sister-in-law's, if it is her.'

'It is. I know it is. She's capable of it too. Maybe I should try to talk to her, reason with her?'

'No, definitely not. We can't approach her, Carmel. She's clearly a very dangerous person if she's willing to go to such lengths. Let's listen to Luke's advice and take it from there.'

They both watched as Joe finished up his conversation with Luke. 'OK, well, if you're sure... I'm sure she'd appreciate it. OK... I'll tell her. Bye, Son. Thanks.' Joe hung up. 'He's coming over in the morning. He's got some contacts in Scotland Yard, and he'll see what's to be done. If it's extortion or blackmail, then that's a crime, obviously, but it's just a matter of proving it. Anyway, he said to tell you to do nothing for now and that he'll see us tomorrow lunchtime.'

'Joe, there was no need for him to drop everything and just come over. I mean, we only rang for a bit of advice.' Carmel was overwhelmed at her brother's generosity.

'He knew you'd say that.' Joe smiled. 'And he said to tell you that there have to be some perks to having a cop in the family, so to take advantage of it and he'll see you tomorrow.' His voice was full of pride, despite the circumstances. 'Now, as he said, in the meantime, the best thing to do is nothing. Just sit tight until we know more. But it's a bit of light at the end of the tunnel, isn't it?'

'It is. Thanks, Joe. Aren't you booked to go back to Ireland in the morning, though?' Sharif was obviously grateful and didn't want to inconvenience him any further.

'I was originally, but I'm after changing my flight to next week. If that's OK? I just want to help you two during this time if I can, and I'd like to spend more time with you, Carmel – if you don't mind, that is. If I'm in the way, please just say it and I'll go back in the morning.'

'Of course you're not in the way –' Carmel began, but Sharif interrupted her.

'We'd love you to stay and we'll need all the support we can get, so if it's not inconveniencing you, then we are delighted. Now, if you're staying, then you must come and stay with us. We have a spare room. What do you think?'

Joe looked at Carmel, the question hanging between them.

'I'd love you to stay with us,' she said. 'I really would.'

'Well, if you're sure.' Joe smiled gratefully.

'We are. Let's go round later and collect your bags, check you out of the hotel and move you in with us.' Carmel shot him a look of gratitude, at least they were able to do that for the man who was throwing him a lifeline.

'Should we still go to Tim's?' Carmel didn't really feel like it, but there was nothing they could do at this stage anyway until Luke got there, so they might as well.

'Sure. I suppose we should, though it's hard to concentrate on it after this. I just wish I'd had the sense to record them – I could have done it with the phone if only I'd have thought. I could kick myself. I was just so angry, listening to them plotting away, that everything else just...'

'Don't worry. We'll get to the bottom of this. At least we now know who is pulling his strings. I always maintained Johnson wasn't sharp enough to come up with all of this on his own.' Sharif paused to think. 'Maybe there is some way out of this mess after all, though I've no idea what. Maybe if we can prove there is a connection between Julia and him or something... I don't know. Imagine being so full of venom that you'd want to destroy someone. She's a piece of work, Carmel – you were right.'

'I would honestly not put anything past her,' Carmel said with conviction. 'She has depths of hatred in her, I don't know from where. But she's capable of this, I'm sure of it. I remember a nasty business a few years ago in the school, or "her school" as she calls it, where a traveller family applied to send their kids there. Of course, Julia wasn't having it, but the family went to the Department of Education and she was more or less compelled to accept them. She didn't like that one bit of course, so she orchestrated a big fight between one of the traveller children and the town bully. That child's father happens to be the town commissioner. She made sure this other child needled and goaded the little traveller kid, saying awful things about his family and all the rest of it. She schooled the bully on exactly what to say – there had been a tragic death in the travelling community the previous year and she knew what buttons to press. Well, of course the traveller child lashed out, and there was a bit of a scrap in the schoolyard. She made it sound and look much worse than it was, and she managed to get the traveller child expelled.'

'She sounds horrendous.' Joe was horrified. 'Don't worry, lads. She'll get her comeuppance, just you watch. First thing will be to find which solicitor in that practice they were going to see, but Luke will advise us about all of that.'

They were a little early for Tim's, so Sharif suggested they go for a coffee. As they walked through the grounds, Joe tried to make sense of it all. 'I mean, if anyone should feel a grievance, it's this Bill character. Not that you owe him anything, but it's his farm that's at stake. Why would his sister go to such lengths? It seems mad.'

'I know it does, but on the other hand, it's perfectly in keeping with her character. I lived under her thumb for long enough.' Carmel wanted them to be under no illusions about who they were dealing with. 'She's poisonous, even where Bill and the girls are concerned, let alone me. Like, I might have had a chance to make a relationship with the twins if she'd have allowed it. And she claims to love them, but I remember Sinead was going with this really nice lad years ago and his family weren't elevated enough in Ballyshanley society, so she told Sinead that he'd cheated on her. Of course he hadn't, but Sinead trusted her aunt so much that she never spoke to the poor fella again. He was heartbroken, and he was such a nice boy. Julia has such notions of herself. Honestly, if you heard her going on, you'd swear Bill's bit of a boggy hillside farm was prime real estate. Nobody in Ballyshanley likes her, and Bill can't bear her, that's the truth, but she wields such power, people are afraid of her. Apparently, years ago, one of the kids in school called her a withered-up auld virgin and she nearly beat the poor lad black and blue. The child's mother was afraid to complain because Julia would take it out on all of the rest of her kids if she did. Julia terrorised the whole town, and because it was the only primary school for miles, people had very few options. She really has a terrible temper. She's said horrible things to children about their families, like that business with the travellers, but she always sucks up to the doctor's kids, the well-to-do in the town. To anyone weak or vulnerable, though, she shows no mercy. And she has such a streak of self-righteousness in her.'

They entered the Aashna coffee shop, full now with patients and staff on their mid-morning break so there were no free tables. In any other situation, someone would have given the boss their table, but nobody did and Sharif would not want them to. He was the owner and the main doctor of Aashna, but the staff treated him just like another co-worker. Carmel loved that he didn't lord his position over anyone.

There was a countertop with high stools along one window with some free space, so they perched there. Carmel went to order, and Lelia, the young woman who ran the coffee shop, said she would drop their drinks over.

Sharif thanked her as she delivered their coffees. 'How is your dad doing now?' he asked.

She sighed. 'All right, Sharif, but he's still limping. Thanks for arranging the referral to the orthopaedic clinic. He says he's fine, but he needs to get checked out. He would never have gone if you hadn't seen how he walked the day he was in here. He's driving my mum daft, though.' She laughed and wiped the table beside them. 'Googling everything. He's diagnosing himself with all sorts now, one extreme to the other.'

Sharif chuckled. He had a sign up in his office that read 'Please do not confuse my medical degree with your Google search' as a joke. He was all for people informing themselves about whatever condition they had, but it drove him daft to have patients and their families quoting crackpot results they got from a Google search at him. 'It's most likely just something easy to fix, but best be sure.' He sipped his coffee.

Lelia went back to serving customers, and the conversation naturally came back to the current situation. They spoke quietly, as they didn't need anyone at Aashna knowing the full story. The staff were loyal and supportive and Sharif was a fair and reasonable employer, but he was essentially a very private person.

'And you really think she's doing this out of badness, or is she after money or what?' Sharif asked, trying to figure out Julia's motivation.

Carmel thought for a moment. She wanted to be as clear-headed as she could in dealing with Julia, to not allow her own prejudiced view of her sister-in-law to cloud her judgement. 'Well, it could be money – she is very greedy. But then she's actually loaded. She hasn't spent a shilling in all the years I've known her. She has a big salary from the government and her parents left her money too, so it's more land and status than actual money that motivates her, I'd say. She's terrified of losing what she sees as her farm. But that greed for land will now be combined with a hatred for me and now you. She never forgets a slight, and she'll see what I did as far more than just a slight. And you backing me puts you in her bad books too, I'm afraid. So to answer your question, money will be a factor, but revenge is more likely the driving force. That's a very dangerous combination. She's got boundless capacity for retribution, and nothing is too much. She's vicious. Nothing would surprise me, even this.'

CHAPTER 27

*J*oe leaned forward and pressed the doorbell beside the lovely ornate Victorian door with the stained-glass panels. The whole place looked like a scene from a picture book, the red brick of the pathway bordered with mosaic tiles, the beautiful wrought-iron gate, painted dark red. Winter blooming cyclamen grew in profusion all around the small but beautiful front garden, and a little fountain trickled in the middle of it all. This was clearly the home of a gardener. Carmel gave her father an encouraging smile as a shadow appeared behind the door.

'Tim, great to see you again.' Joe's greeting was effusive to hide the trepidation he obviously felt.

'Hi Joe, and Carmel. So glad you could come. It's lovely to see you both. Come in.' Tim opened the door wide and they entered.

The house from the outside was like others on the street, detached with a double-bow front but modest in size. Carmel thought it absolutely gorgeous. She'd been there several times since the morning Brian died. That day, her sole focus was on breaking the news to Tim and being there for him, but on subsequent visits, she had time to take it all in, and she thought the home was like a picture you'd see in a child's story book or one of those ads off the TV at Christmas. The décor was tasteful and unique, nothing like what one would expect in the home of two bachelors in their seventies. The tiles on the floor were terracotta and well worn, which gave the house a lovely rustic charm, and there was no clutter, no hallstand filled with jackets and outdoor shoes; instead, the house was calm and unfussy. The hallway was painted a dove grey with what looked like hand-painted birds of paradise here and there. Coloured light flooded the space through an ornate stained-glass skylight overhead, and straight in front of them were distressed-pine double doors leading to a large open-plan kitchen and dining room that looked onto an amazing back garden. Tim had said that he and Brian spent years planning and decorating their home, and it reflected them both. They watched those home improvement TV shows all the time, and Tim had become sad when he told her how Brian loved *Escape to the Sun*, in which people bought property in holiday locations. The way he described their life together made Carmel's heart ache. To the outside world, Brian was Tim's tenant, but once inside the door, there was no doubt how much they meant to each other.

'I hope you haven't eaten? I've made supper.' Tim smiled shyly, and Carmel knew at once he was as nervous as Joe.

She wondered if she should have called him ahead of arriving, given him some indication that Joe knew the truth about his relationship with Brian, but she'd decided against it. She trusted Joe to be gentle with him and to let the story emerge in its own time. 'We haven't, not that we were expecting it. We were planning on going to the pub afterwards, but this smells divine.' Carmel was touched he'd gone to so much trouble.

'It's just chicken in white wine and some new spuds. I don't bother cooking much these days, so it's nice to have the excuse.' The pain at the loss of

Brian was clearly as raw as it had been at the funeral, but they could tell he was doing his best.

'It's a gorgeous place you have here, the house and the garden. It's like a little oasis of peace in the hustle and bustle.' Joe looked around, admiring everything.

'Well, I'm into interior design a bit, more the DIY side than the design really, I suppose, but the garden was all Brian. He would spend hours out there, doing God knows what. I'm clueless, wouldn't know a dahlia from a daisy.'

Joe chuckled. 'I'm exactly the same. Give me a hammer or a drill and I'm happy as Larry, but everything I plant I manage to kill, even the stuff they assure me I can't destroy. I seem to have the knack. We didn't have a garden growing up, so I wonder how Brian got so good at it?' Joe gazed in admiration at the back garden.

There was a little seating area with paving slabs and coloured stone chippings, a barbeque and a firepit, and all around the perimeter of the garden was an undulating shrub bed, red robin and evergreen shrubs lent it a splash of colour. It was yellow-brick-lined, and the whole space seemed to be coordinated. The entire back of the house was glass, so the effect was spectacular. It felt like the garden was almost part of the house.

'Apparently,' Tim explained as he took the cast-iron casserole dish from the oven, 'when he came over to London first, he was trying to make a life here, I suppose, and he was working and all of that, but he took a night class in the local secondary school. In fact, he signed up to do landscape painting, but he showed up on the night of gardening class by mistake and decided he'd stay at it. It's just as well, really, since he turned out to have very green fingers but couldn't draw a straight line! I doubt painting would have worked out so well.' Tim chuckled.

Maybe it was because she knew what they meant to each other, but Carmel felt there was something proprietary in the way Tim spoke about Brian, something intimate and special. Her heart broke for his loss.

'Now, can I get you a drink? A glass of wine?'

'I'd love a glass of white, please,' Carmel said.

She loved Tim's house. It was so elegant and restful. The huge range cooker built into the island at the centre of the room, the bleached wood table with fabulous carved benches on either side. She could imagine how happy Tim and Brian had been there.

'I'd love a glass of anything, Tim. I'm not fussy.' Joe smiled his thanks.

Tim opened a bottle of Riesling, and they sat on high stools around the kitchen island, the sun setting over the garden outside. They sat in companionable silence for a moment, and then Joe held up his drink. 'This is such a beautiful home you two made, and such a magnificent garden. I've never seen its equal, and I've been in a lot of houses. I can see exactly why my brother dropped anchor here. To Brian.'

'To Brian.' Carmel and Tim clinked glasses.

'So you know?' Tim asked quietly, staring at the floor between his feet.

Joe sat back and sighed. 'I do. Carmel told me last night. I can't say I had any inkling before, and I'll be honest that I was a bit sad that he never felt he could tell me. He surely didn't think I'd mind? But I'm very glad he had such a great life.' Joe took a sip of his wine and gazed at Tim, whose head was still down. 'Such a great love.'

Long seconds passed before Tim spoke quietly, never lifting his head. 'He didn't tell you because of me. It was something that caused him great pain – I know it did – keeping who he was secret from all of you. But he knew that my kids could never accept our relationship, so he didn't tell anyone. I'd hate to think you were hurt that he didn't say anything to you. He definitely would have told you if my situation were different. He did that for me. He never doubted for a minute that you all would be accepting and supportive. The split from my ex-wife was very bitter. She had every reason to be – I married her knowing I couldn't love her, not the way she should be loved. That destroys a person over the years. When she finally found out the reason I wasn't a proper husband to her, she...well, she couldn't bear the shame of anyone knowing so made me promise to never reveal to anyone who I really was. Giving in to her request was the only thing I could do to lessen that pain I'd caused, so I promised.'

'And your children, they still don't know you're gay?' Joe caught Carmel's eye. She'd had an inkling that was the reason but nothing concrete.

'No, they don't, and it will have to stay that way. Their mother is still alive, and well...I gave her my word. I've kept it up this long – it won't be so bad to keep it up for the rest of my life at this stage. To be totally honest with you, I'm not entirely sure what the point of my life is any more. My children are grown up, and while I love them, they've got their own lives to live. I see them every few weeks but...it's so lonely without

Brian. I miss him so much.' His voice choked on the last admission.

Joe leaned over and placed his hand on Tim's. It was a strange gesture, Carmel thought, for two Irish men of their age, but it was the right thing to do.

'I miss him too. He was always there for me as well. Every day, especially these last few weeks, I've instinctively gone to ring him, and then it hits me again that he's gone. It makes me feel better now that I know the reason he never said anything. Brian was that kind – if he made you a promise, he stuck to it, no exceptions. I presume you know all about Dolly and all that story?'

'I do. It was hard on him. He tried everything to get her to tell you the truth, but she was adamant. Between me and her, we put a lot on his shoulders in terms of secrets. Another man might have buckled under the pressure, or just felt it was the right thing to tell the truth, but Brian wasn't like that.'

Tim topped up their glasses, and an easy silence descended once more, with each lost in their own thoughts. Carmel eventually spoke. 'I can understand why she didn't want to tell Joe, especially after what happened to her. And as far as she was concerned, I was lost, so she didn't see the point of disrupting your life for nothing. But I like to think that if Sharif had found me when she was still alive, then we would have found you and told you the truth. Either way, I think both Dolly and Brian would be glad to see how things have turned out.'

The two men nodded. Carmel then turned to Tim. 'Joe and I have decided – well, I'm not sure what the term is, but anyway, we've made the decision that he's my dad and I'm delighted he is.' Carmel looked at Joe and thought how she could never get enough of his twinkly smile.

'So you've had the test?' Tim seemed surprised.

'No. And I'm not going to. What we have is perfect. We have found each other and want to be in each other's lives, and finding out that he isn't my biological father would be so hurtful and hard, especially given the situation. I think we'll let that information stay with the dead, where it belongs. Joe's extended family, and Jennifer and Luke, have all been amazing and so welcoming. For me, this is just perfect.'

A dark cloud threatened the evening sky, and they saw the first specks of rain slide down the glass but they were cosy inside. The aromas were mouth-watering, and Carmel found she was really hungry. It had been such a bizarre day, and she had only had a few cups of coffee so far.

THEY CHATTED EASILY over the succulent creamy chicken, minted peas that were from the garden, Tim told them, and crispy potatoes, their skins caramelised expertly. And they even laughed. Tim showed them a photo album, normally kept hidden from view, of holidays he and Brian had taken together, where they could be less formal than they were in England. While there weren't pictures of them kissing or holding hands or anything like that, there was an undeniable closeness there. Brian was handsome in the photos, and Carmel felt sad that she'd only seen her uncle in the last stages of cancer when that cruel disease had stripped his bones of flesh and diminished what was once a powerful physique. He'd had a full head of hair, dark and slightly longer than most men wore, and dressed casually in t-shirts and shorts. She could see why Tim fell for him.

As Joe turned the pages slowly, he spoke to Tim. 'Lots of people go their whole lives without a love like that. I know the pain of losing him is tearing you apart now, but it will get better, and soon the memories will keep you company and it won't seem that bad – or at least it becomes bearable.'

CHAPTER 28

Carmel marvelled at how Joe was so intuitive about what people needed. She thought he would make such a good counsellor. He had empathy and kindness and yet was fundamentally a jovial kind of man.

'Were you like this after your wife died?' Tim asked.

Joe thought about his answer. 'Yes and no. Mary, she was a great mother and wife, and I miss her every day. We had such a great marriage, open, respectful, loving, and she was great craic as well. But I'll be honest – the greatest loss I ever had in my life was Dolly. Even now, all these years later, I think about her. Carmel showed me a video, the one taken at her birthday party at

Aashna House, and even though a lifetime had passed and time had done its work as it does on us all, there she was, my Dolly, still the same, the same glint of mischief in her eye. She was a rogue, that one. If there was blackguarding going on, you could be sure Dolly would be stuck in the middle of it all. At least she was before...' A darkness crossed his face. 'She was like a tiger, so loyal and fierce. That's why it must have almost killed her that she couldn't get you back, Carmel.'

Carmel sat with these two men, people she never knew existed a year earlier, and felt a profound sense of connection to them.

They chatted all evening about Brian, Tim filling them in on their life in London, Joe telling stories about him and Brian growing up together in Dublin. It was a warm and gentle evening, and it did both men good to reminisce.

'So what now for you, Tim? Have you any plans?' Carmel asked gently.

'I don't know, really. Brian and I had an idea to rent this place out, maybe go travelling for a few months. He wanted to go to Norway to see the Northern Lights, and I wanted to see the migration of the butterflies to Mexico, so we had a bucket list. Unfortunately, Brian decided to kick that before we got to live out our plans.' He shrugged. 'I suppose I'll have to go back to Mayo sometime, though that thought doesn't exactly delight me, to be honest. There's land and a farm there that I own, and I honestly don't know what's happening with it. I was an only child and so the farm came to me. A local farmer is using the land, I believe, but as for the house, I don't know. I don't relish it.'

'Why not?' Joe asked. The intimacy and friendship of the evening meant the question wasn't impertinent. They'd shared so much.

Tim sat back and paused for a moment, clearly deciding whether or not to tell them. He eyed each of them before speaking. 'My father caught myself and a local lad in the barn one night, so many years ago now. Such behaviour was not to be tolerated at all to his mind, let alone in a son of his. Anyway, he threw me out and told me never to come back again, ever. As far as he was concerned, I was dead and that was the best thing for everyone. He didn't soften or waver as far as I know, so I took him at his word and I didn't go back to Ireland while he was alive. The only time I've gone back across the Irish Sea was to my mother's funeral, but that was over twenty-seven years ago. Ireland is no place for someone like me. I'm happy here in London.'

'I know how you feel,' Carmel agreed. 'Ireland isn't exactly calling me either. If I never go there again, it will suit me just fine.'

'Ah, now, you're both being a bit harsh on the old sod, if you don't mind me saying so.' Joe seemed genuinely indignant.

Carmel gave a rueful smile. 'Well, maybe Ireland was kinder to you than it was to either of us.' The look on his face told her that her words had hurt him, and she felt instantly regretful.

'Well, the very same bigotry you describe allowed my father to beat my mother and my brothers and sisters, it allowed my girl to be raped with no consequences for the perpetrator and her to be imprisoned, and for our child to be taken from us, so I'm not exactly unscarred either. But Ireland is many things. Was it mean-spirited and church-ridden for too long? Certainly. But are the people bad generally? Of course not. Don't blame a whole country for the wrongdoing of a few.'

'I'm sorry, Joe, I didn't mean –' Carmel began.

'It's all right, love. I'm not saying you didn't suffer, or that it's some kind of competition as to who had the hardest time. All I'm saying is that you are both Irish and you each had your own very valid reasons for leaving, but it's not fair to blame the whole flippin' country. Seriously, Tim, you'd see lads and girls walking down Grafton Street on a Saturday afternoon, holding hands and canoodling of all kinds, straight, gay, transgender, gender-fluid – whatever the hell that is, I don't know. But the point is, the Ireland you left was a very different place. We were the first country in the world to legalise gay marriage by popular vote – you saw that on the news – and people are kinder. There was nothing good about the good auld days, certainly, but it's a very different place now. And from what I know of Mayo nowadays, it's all café culture and craft beers and fellas wearing shorts and going sailing. I think you'd be very surprised, but in a good way.'

Tim held his hands up in capitulation. 'OK, OK... I never anticipated a Bord Fáilte representative! The tourist board should recruit you.'

'Well, I just love my country and think you're letting one bad experience colour your view of the whole place. And as for you, young lady' – he pointed at Carmel, mock stern – 'Ireland is your home, it's in your blood, and no matter what, you need to reconcile yourself with that. You're coming over for Aisling's wedding – why don't we make a little holiday of it, travel round a bit? I bet you've never even seen the west coast, have you? Tell her, Tim, is there anywhere nicer in the entire world than the west coast of Ireland on a summer's evening?'

Tim nodded. 'He's right, Carmel. I can't argue with that. It's like paradise, the crashing waves, the green hills rolling to the sea, tumble-down old castles beside white painted cottages, bright till eleven o'clock at night, and then watching the orange sun sink below the horizon of the Atlantic. I miss that all right.'

'Hey, why don't you come too, Tim? We could all go together, rent a big people carrier and drive out west, stay in little B and Bs and explore our country. You could sort out whatever you need to do with your homeplace, and at least it would be in the company of friends, maybe less sad. God knows, enough tourists do it every year, and there we are, Irish people, and we not taking advantage of the bit of heaven on earth God chose to land us in. We're lucky people. I know it's hard, and life has been tough for all of us at one time or another. I'm not diminishing it. But there's something soothing to the soul about standing on the soil of your own land, watching the seabirds nest on the big cliffs, drinking a pint of Guinness and eating fresh fish while a bunch of hairy fellas belt

THE FUTURE'S NOT OURS TO SEE

out tunes on pipes and fiddles. Come on – are you with me?'

Carmel and Tim both burst out laughing at Joe's impromptu sales pitch.

'Well, are you coming or what?' His face was like a child's, full of enthusiasm and fun.

'Fine, OK, yes, I'll come,' Tim agreed.

'Carmel? There's no backing out now if you say yes. Sharif will love it, and he needs a holiday.' Joe was determined, and Carmel knew he wouldn't accept procrastination.

'Yes, I'd love to drink a pint of Guinness, the first of my life, with you two somewhere in Ireland.'

'Great! I'll book it all when I get back and let you know the dates. March sometime, OK? Would Nadia come, do you think?'

Carmel laughed at the thought of them all, bouncing around the west of Ireland. 'Well, I don't know, but you can ask her. I'm getting the feeling you're a hard man to refuse.'

Tim smiled, and for a moment, Carmel could see the pain of his loss had dulled a little.

CHAPTER 29

*L*uke landed at Luton the following afternoon, and Joe went to pick him up. They all met, along with Nadia, in Carmel and Sharif's flat. As usual, Nadia brought some amazing-smelling pastries.

'If we are having a council of war, then an army marches on its stomach and we'll be no exception.' She smiled, but there was steely determination behind it all. Nobody threatened her son and got away with it.

Carmel was surprised at how Luke's demeanour had changed. Gone was the jokey semi-student, replaced by a serious law enforcement professional.

'OK, so what we're looking at is blackmail, and that's an offence under Section 21 of the Theft Act 1968. Basically, it means someone making an unwarranted demand with menace, with a view to making a gain or causing a loss.'

'Which is exactly what Johnson is doing.' Nadia was adamant. 'And this Julia woman. I wonder if he had this idea and she spurred him on or if it was all her doing? She is definitely the brains of the operation. Johnson has been moaning for ages, but going to a solicitor, the photos – he's not smart enough to do all of that on his own. And how did they meet? It seems so odd that she from Ireland would know this Derek Johnson.'

Sharif spoke up. 'I wondered that too. I got a few key members of staff together this morning to fill them in on what's happening. I don't want it broadcast, obviously, but we have a great team here, so I spoke with them. Johnson was complaining long before Julia arrived, but we do know they had a conversation on the day Julia appeared in Aashna House. Oscar mentioned that Johnson was in the car park, complaining about everything again. He stormed off on Carmel earlier that day, but he must have come back later.

Julia went over to him and started a conversation. She was on her way out after I more or less threw her out of here. Oscar thought nothing of it until I told him what was going on.'

'Well, yes, that makes sense.' Luke was thinking aloud. 'She's got a grudge against you, Carmel, and now Sharif as well. She thinks you're behind Carmel wanting a divorce, and Johnson was the willing stick she could use to beat you with. That's almost certainly the truth, but proving it is the tricky bit. I spoke to my opposite number in Scotland Yard off the record this morning, and he was of the same opinion as me – to just wait and see what happens. Do nothing.' He noted their faces. 'Look, I know it's so frustrating just to watch and wait, but he's claiming that his mother was badly treated and he has some evidence, however fraudulently achieved, to that effect. As Sharif has been advised, malpractice suits are notoriously hard to fight and very costly. You could pursue them through the law, and you should, I suppose, as they are engaging in criminality, but this is the brother, not the cop speaking – it's a long drawn-out process and all the reputational effect of all that negative publicity could never be quantified.'

'Well, what about we play her at her own game?' Nadia's dark eyes flashed with fury. 'I mean, she's a school principal over in Ireland, for God's sake. Surely she won't want her employers to know what sort of thing she's involved with over here. We could threaten to expose her.'

'I know why you feel like that, Nadia, but honestly, Sharif has the high moral ground here – he's done nothing wrong. If we threaten her, or make any suggestion of blackmailing her, then it becomes a tit-for-tat thing and that's much murkier from a legal perspective.' Luke was the voice of reason.

'But, Luke, I heard them plotting. Surely they can't just get away with this – it's not right.' Joe was getting aggravated.

'I understand that, Dad, and if this wasn't family, I'd probably be saying get straight down to the local cop shop, but I know how these things work. They are taking, or threatening to take, a civil case. In essence, by involving the police, you are turning this into a criminal case. So you'd effectively be upping the ante on something that you really just want to disappear. Do you see what I mean? They haven't escalated it yet, and maybe they'll never have the guts to actually go through with it. The evidence is very flimsy, and I'm sure any new solicitor would tell them that. I think Johnson's hoping you'll just pay up and then he'll scurry off into the corner. As for Julia, well, she just wants to break you both. You can call their bluff, certainly, say, sure, let's see how this plays out in court, but then you're back into negative publicity, no smoke without fire and all of that. And with hospitals and doctors, there are always more moaners willing to jump on the bandwagon, some other person's family who sees a chance to strike gold. And to add to it, if the legal end of things doesn't work out for him, he could just send the photos to an unscrupulous daily rag and they'll print them. It's rotten, I know, but it's how it is.'

'So is your advice just to pay them off?' Sharif spoke for the first time.

'My advice, and that of my colleague over here, is just to sit tight and see what they do next. They've sent the letter to your solicitor, along with the photographs. They never made a demand. Now we know from what Dad overheard that the first solicitor is after dumping them. Clearly he or she realises this is fraud so had the good sense to put the run on them. Most solicitors won't even take this kind of thing on. Of course, there are some sleazeballs who will, but it might be tougher than they think. So my advice is to wait. See what happens next. I know it's hard and it's a worry hanging over you, but if it were me, that's what I'd do.'

Clearly neither Nadia nor Joe was happy. They were both indignant and with good reason. That someone as unscrupulous as Johnson, and now Julia, could just throw a grenade into Sharif and Carmel's lives out of spite was infuriating.

'I appreciate what you're saying, Luke.' Nadia was so furious it was palpable. 'And I know on one level it makes sense, but even if they can't get another solicitor to take a legal case on their be-half, what if they just email the photos off to the local paper? We are ruined then, either way. I just hate that they hold all the cards.'

Sharif looked shaken, and Carmel knew he was ruminating on what Luke had told them. Luke was the best authority they had, he and the solicitor, both of whom were now suggesting that they sit tight and hope that things died down. She knew that taking such a passive approach wasn't in Sharif's nature; he didn't get his place up and running by taking adversity lying down. There were many hurdles to cross in those days, and he went at each one head on. This was killing him.

As the conversation went on around her, Carmel took it all in. These people had given her a happy, love-filled life, something she never imagined she could ever have. She knew what she had to do.

CHAPTER 30

'*A dhaoine uaisle, tá failte roimh go leir to Baile Atha Cliath.* Ladies and gentlemen, you are all very welcome to Dublin. We hope you enjoyed your flight and look forward to welcoming you on board another Aer Lingus flight very soon. In the meantime, *Slan agus beannacht.*'

Carmel hadn't heard Irish spoken in months, and even though she wasn't brilliant at it when she was at school, it still was nice to hear. Maybe Joe was right – Ireland wasn't to blame for her life and she shouldn't write off the whole country. She stood up to retrieve her carry-on bag from the overhead bin. She'd never flown before, but she was figuring it out.

She showed her passport and was waved

through security, and within moments, she was in the terminal building. She made her way to the bus ticket kiosk and purchased an expressway ticket into the city centre. She'd have to start from there.

The streets seemed so familiar and yet so alien to her now. The reflection of her face in the bus window blended with the buildings on the way to the main bus station. She marvelled at how cosmopolitan Dublin had become. Though she had grown up there, she rarely had reason to venture into the city as a child, and since marrying Bill, she'd come to the capital only three or four times. The last time she was there was the first time she met Sharif, and then, well, after that everything changed.

He'd be up by now, would have seen her note begging him not to worry, assuring him she'd call later that night. She'd turned her phone off because she knew once he realised what she was going to do, or where she was going, he'd try to talk her out of it, but she was sure, surer than she'd ever been about anything, that this was the only way out of the mess Sharif and Aashna House were in.

The familiar accents and sounds and smells of Ireland assaulted her senses as she waited in line for another ticket. The central bus station was a hive of activity, and all human life was there: students engrossed in smartphones, earphones jammed in their ears; mothers trying to control unruly toddlers; elderly ladies on day trips, availing of the free travel for all pensioners the Irish government supplied; and of course a good smattering of tourists.

'Next,' the bored-looking woman called from behind the glass.

Carmel stepped forward. 'Ballyshanley, please.'

'Single or return?'

'Single…I mean, return. I thought you meant was I single. Return. I'd like a return, please…' Carmel mumbled, feeling her face redden in embarrassment.

'One day, three day or twenty-one day?'

'Pardon? Sorry, I don't unders –'

'Do you want to come back today? In three days? Or in three weeks?' The woman spoke slowly and loudly, clearly used to dealing with all sorts of people.

'Er…I don't know…it depends…em…'

The woman eyeballed her, exuding disdain and frustration from every pore.

'I'll just take a one-day return, I think,' Carmel eventually said weakly.

'Eleven seventy.' The woman tapped some things into a computer and a ticket was generated.

Carmel paid and took her ticket. 'Do you know where the bus leaves from?'

The woman pointed at a gigantic screen indicating which bus left from which lane.

'Oh, right, thanks…'

She was putting everything back into her purse when the woman yelled, 'Next,' and Carmel shuffled away, trying to close her purse as she went.

She examined the board for quite a while, finally finding the bay and bus number she needed. She grabbed a bottle of water and a chocolate bar in the little shop, then made her way to the bus, secretly begging her mother to make sure there was nobody there she recognised. She'd been doing that a lot lately, not that she'd admit it to anyone, but it gave her comfort. When she saw robins or feathers on the ground, Carmel felt her mother's presence and was convinced her mother's spirit was with her. It gave her strength.

Thankfully, she was one of the first to take her place in the queue and found a seat at the very back, minimising the chances of being seen. She had to change buses at Birr and take another bus to Ballyshanley. Once she arrived in the village, she didn't exactly have a plan. The farm was three miles outside the town, and there wasn't a bus. On her once-weekly trips for grocery shopping, she took the weekly community bus that took all the elderly people into town, to the clinic, to the library or for a few messages. But that bus only went on Wednesdays and it was Friday.

She wished she knew where Julia was. The school was off for the holidays so she probably wasn't there. She may well still have been in England. Carmel hoped she was.

The journey was uneventful, and she tried not to look too guilty or conspicuous as she got off the bus in the square. She prayed again to meet no acquaintance. It was hard enough being back. Everything looked so familiar, the shops, the streets, but she wasn't that person any more; she was someone else.

Gripping her overnight bag, she made her way west of the town, passing the entrance to Ballyshanley Castle. She remembered how she used to watch the families gather for picnics there often. The riverside walk was lovely, grounds nestled in the lee of the ruined castle walls. There was a playground, and she'd some-times sit near it and wonder what it was like to have children. Couples walking hand in hand, fa-thers carrying little kids on their shoulders, friends power-walking and gossiping – all of it was right in front of her but might as well have been on Mars for all she knew about it. She'd been on the outside looking in her whole life, until now. How she longed to be back in London with Sharif, safe and loved, but she needed to be here. He'd done so much for her. He had given her a chance at happiness, and she owed him this.

The sun was high in the sky as she walked, and her bag felt much heavier than it had when she crept out of the apartment at five that morn-ing. Sharif had been in the clinic all night as the teenage girl with leukaemia was dying. Debbie's parents and little brothers were distraught, and Sharif was there as much for them as for Debbie.

Carmel climbed the hill and saw their house, or Bill's house as she always thought of it, in front of her. His car was parked outside as usual; he didn't like to drive it into the yard in case it got dirty. Bill was very particular about his car.

'Okay, Dolly.' She spoke to herself. 'If I ever needed you, I need you now. Firstly, keep that witch Julia away. Whatever hope I have of managing this without her here, I'll have none at all if she turns up.'

It was as if ice were churning in the pit of her stomach. The chocolate she ate on the bus was the only food she'd taken, and she was light-headed. This was insane – what was she doing here?

'Calm, Carmel. Use your breath to steady yourself. You can do this.' She repeated the mantra to herself as she approached the house. What should she do? Knock on the door? Go around the back? The back door was usually not locked. Or should she just take the spare key from under the milk churn with flowers in it and open the front door?

Eventually, she decided to knock on the back door. She didn't even know if he'd be there, but there was a chance. With trembling hands, she made a fist and knocked. Nothing. She was about to knock again when she saw the shape of someone through the bubble glass, and the door opened.

CHAPTER 31

'Hello, Bill,' was all she managed.
He stood there for a long moment just looking at her, then turned back into the house, leaving the door open. Assuming she could go in, she stepped inside to the back kitchen and followed him into the main room of the farmhouse. Everything was exactly the same – the décor, the ornaments, the Waterford Crystal-framed wedding photo of Bill and Gretta. The only thing different was a kind of sour smell, like the place needed a good clean.

He stood with his back to the range, his hands in his pockets. She thought he looked old and tired. He needed a haircut and had cut himself shaving; there was blood on the collar of his shirt.

'Are you coming back?' he asked, eyeing her small bag.

'I...I... Well, no, I'm not, but I just wanted to talk to you, in person...face to face, you know?'

'About what?' His voice was leaden.

Carmel took a breath; clearly, he wasn't going to engage in small talk. 'I'm sorry I left you the way I did. I should have said something. It was wrong of me.'

He looked at her, clearly taking in her new clothes and hair. She was sure she looked like a different person. Not just looks either – she was a different person.

'It was,' he said.

'And so I want to say I'm sorry.'

'So your fancy man, that darkie, he kicked you out, did he?'

Carmel tried not to flinch at the racist description of Sharif. She couldn't let this turn into a fight. 'No, no, he didn't.'

'So what are you doing here?'

'I wanted to talk.'

'About what?'

'About us, about the future.' She took a deep breath. 'About Julia.'

Again the silence, his eyes raking her face for a clue. The clock ticked on the mantlepiece, and she felt her chest constrict with anxiety.

'There's nothing you can say to me that I'd care to hear,' Bill said wearily. 'Your solicitor and mine will be hammering out the details, but don't be expecting much. This is my land, and I won't be giving it up, for you or for anyone else for that matter.'

Carmel thought it might have been one of the longest sentences he'd ever addressed at her. 'Well…if you'd just hear me out anyway.'

Carmel was doing her very best to stay neutral and reasonable; Bill would baulk immediately if she started crying or got upset. This was her only chance; she had to take it and make the best effort she could. 'Sharif knew my birth mother. That's why he came to see me, to give me some letters she wrote to me. She never wanted to give me up, but she was raped, you see, and she had no choice. The man who raped her insisted that I never be adopted, and so I never was. When I met you, I really hoped I could be part of your life, your family, but I wasn't, I couldn't. I did try – I swear to you, I did. I wanted to be a mother to Sinead and Niamh, but there just wasn't room for me.'

She tried to see if there was any hint of understanding or anything at all on his face, but he just stood there, hands still in his pockets, his expression giving nothing away.

'I...I was so lonely, Bill. I...wanted you to love me, but to be honest, I wasn't sure you even liked me. You married me, and for years I wondered why. Until that day you told me it was to stop Julia moving in.'

The silence between them was thick and heavy. If he refused to speak now, then she might have blown it. Just as she was beginning to think he was never going to reply, that she'd have to take her bag and leave, he spoke. 'Do you want money? Is that it? Because I'll give you money if you don't go after the farm.' She thought she heard some emotion in his voice, but she couldn't be sure.

'Bill, listen to me. I don't want your money or your farm. I don't want one single penny from you.'

'Your solicitor does.' He sounded petulant.

'Well, I don't, and he works for me. He was just doing what is standard practice. I'm with Sharif now and we have enough money. I just want us both to move on with our lives and try to be happy.'

Carmel looked at Bill; he looked so much

older than his fifty-four years. She felt a sudden surge of almost affection for this man whom she'd called her husband for all those years but was, in fact, a total stranger to her.

'Bill, can we sit down?' She kept her voice gentle, not wanting to break the spell. She moved to the kitchen table and pulled out two chairs.

He sat down, and she sat opposite him. Her voice was steady and confident, infused with kindness. 'Gretta was the love of your life, and sometimes you only get one of those.'

He looked up at her and sighed, nodding slowly, as if not trusting himself to speak. After a pause, he said, 'And this fella, is he that for you?' Bill's blue eyes were locked with hers.

If she was to have any hope of getting him to understand, then this was it. 'I think so, yes. I love him, Bill, and he loves me.'

More silence.

'Right so. That's it.' He started to get up.

'But, Bill, there's something else.'

'What?' He was wary again, and any shred of intimacy dissipated.

'I don't want anything from you, I swear. I know I've hurt you or embarrassed you or something, and I'm truly sorry for that, but I just want us to divorce and get on with our lives.'

'Fine. Send whatever papers you need me to sign.' He stood.

'Julia is blackmailing us.' She blurted it out, fearful he was going to leave and the chance would be lost.

'What?' He turned, his brow furrowed.

'It's a long story, but Sharif is a doctor and owns a private hospice in England. There is a man trying to claim that Sharif isn't taking proper care of his mother, an elderly patient. It's lies, of course, but Julia is involved. She is going to solicitors, and she got him to take photos of his mother in dirty sheets and with ashtrays all around and all of that, totally fabricated. She wants to hurt me and Sharif. She came over a while ago, threatening me to leave the farm alone, and things got a bit heated. She was so angry, and she wants to hurt us. I know you probably don't believe me, but I have witnesses who have over-heard her plotting with this man...' Carmel knew she was getting overexcited in her efforts to have him believe her, but she was frightened he'd just dismiss her and walk out the door.

Bill sat back down, clearly thinking. Carmel stopped talking. She knew that he'd only say something when there was space to say it.

He sighed deeply, obviously tired of it all. 'We

had words. She told me all about your set-up when she came back from England. I didn't know she was going over there – I wouldn't have allowed it had I known. She's had too much to do with me and the girls since Gretta died. Gretta couldn't stick her, actually. Julia was full of bile for you and your man, saying this and that. To be honest I didn't want to hear it, and then she rounded on me, saying I wasn't man enough to stand up to you and that you'd made a show of me and all of that.'

Carmel couldn't believe her ears. 'Did she say anything about doing this thing to hurt us?' Carmel didn't want to interrupt his flow, but she was so unsure as to how to handle this new verbose Bill that she decided to strike while the iron was hot.

'No. As I said, we haven't spoken since that day.'

'Could you try to talk to her now? I know I've no right to ask you for anything after what I did, but Sharif has worked his whole life to build that place up from nothing. You get that, don't you? If someone threatened the farm, you'd have to fight back? And it really is such a special place, and it seems that malpractice suits are so hard to fight...'

He just sat there, and it was impossible to know if he was absorbing what she'd said or not. Finally he spoke. 'That's very wrong, what she's doing. She's a spiteful woman, always was.' Without saying another word he stood, crossed the room and picked up the phone, which was attached to the wall. He consulted the little brown address book he kept hanging beside it on a piece of twine. As he punched in a number, Carmel wondered, hardly daring to breathe, about what was going to come next.

'Julia? It's Bill.' A pause. 'Yes, I am, of course, at home. Where else would I be?' Another pause, then he spoke, the irritation in his voice unmistakable. 'Listen to me now, and stop your blathering. I know what you're up to with that fella you met over in England, trying to tell a load of lies about that hospital or whatever it is. Now listen carefully. If you ever want to speak to me or the girls ever again, you stop this right this minute. And find some way of stopping that other fool you're after getting yourself tangled up with. Do you hear me?'

There was a long silence while he listened. 'That's your own business. You got yourself into this, and you may get yourself out of it. I am warning you that this is to stop unless you want the whole place here to know what you're at, and that includes Father Linehan, who is the chairman of the board of management of the school above, and Father Creedon as well – and you know well he's only looking for any excuse to go after you. You've plenty of enemies who'd only be too happy to see you brought down, so think on that.'

Another silence. 'Won't I? Well, you'll just have to wait and see about that now.' And he hung up.

Carmel was astounded. On so many levels.

'Right. She'll call it off. Now, I've to go. I've calves coming and two cows with mastitis.' He took his coat from the back of the door.

'Bill.'

He turned. Did she imagine a softness in his old careworn face? Possibly.

'Thanks. It means the world to me that you helped me out. And I'm sorry. I really, really am.'

He stopped, and for a moment, she thought he was just going to leave without another word, but he turned and crossed the room and stood in front of her. She could almost see him formulating the words in his head. Eventually, he spoke. ''Tis I should be sorry, dragging a young girl in here and being…well…not right. And that day when you asked me why I married you, well, I was a bit harsh. I'm not one for much chat, but I could have made things nicer for you. Gretta would be very vexed with me for the way I treated you, so I'm sorry too. I hope you'll be happy.' He held his hand out to shake hers, the only voluntary touch in nearly two decades of marriage.

She ignored it and leaned in and kissed him on the cheek. 'I wish you happiness too, Bill. I really do.'

He nodded. 'Will I run you down to the bus in the car?'

'That would be great, thanks.'

They pulled away from the house for what Carmel knew would be the very last time. She didn't look back; there was nothing to see.

CHAPTER 32

'Good afternoon, ladies and gentlemen, and you are all very welcome aboard this flight EI 348 to London Luton. Please ensure your tray tops are secure, seats upright and seat belts fastened. Our flight time today is fifty-five minutes...'

Carmel switched her phone back on for a moment and wrote a text to Sharif and Joe. As she expected, there were several missed calls from both of them.

Hi. Am OK. See you later, will explain then. C x

She switched it off again. This wasn't a conversation she could have over the phone, and anyway, she just needed some time with her thoughts.

Luckily, there was a flight back to London that evening, and she'd bought a ticket, smiling to herself at how competent a traveller she had become in just a few short months. She dozed on the flight and only woke to the bump as the plane touched down.

The taxi dropped her at reception of Aashna House, and even though it had only been a day, it felt different. She hoped Sharif was there; she needed to see him.

'Oh, Carmel, hi! We were starting to worry. Sharif has been in and out all day asking if you were back yet.' Marlena smiled. She was getting ready to leave for the night. 'Well, he was until this evening. Mrs Johnson has gone down rapidly – he's with her now. Will I beep him for you?'

'No, no, that's OK, Marlena. I'll find him. I don't want to disturb him if he's with a patient. Er...is Mrs Johnson's son there?' Carmel lowered her voice, even though the entire area was empty.

'No. He was here this afternoon. Seems he took a lot of her things, jewellery and so on, and left. The staff told him that the end was close – she's been in and out of consciousness all day really – but he didn't seem to care. He didn't even say goodbye to her, and now he's not picking up his phone.' Marlena's normally perfectly professional demeanour slipped a little. 'He is so awful, that Johnson man. Really horrid.'

'Yep, you're not wrong there,' Carmel said wearily.

She made her way to Mrs Johnson's room, deciding she would just peek in. If Sharif was attending to her, then she would leave and wait for him at home, but he could just be sitting with her. He was insistent that nobody should leave this earth alone, so when patients had nobody, it was often Sharif who held their hand as they took their last breath.

It was late now and most of the night staff were on, but they were quiet and the lights were dimmed. The door to Mrs Johnson's room was slightly ajar, and as she had suspected, there he was, sitting beside her bed, her small hand in his.

He looked up as she entered and sighed. 'You're back,' he whispered. 'I was worried.'

She kissed the top of his head and sat beside him. 'I'm sorry. I went to Ireland to see Bill. I asked him to speak to Julia, to call this whole thing off.'

Sharif turned and gazed intently at her. 'And?'

'And he did what I asked. He told her to stop everything or she'd never see him or the girls again, and he threatened to report her to the board of management of the school. He also told her to find a way to get Derek Johnson to withdraw his case as well.'

'Really?' Sharif's brow was knitted in confusion. 'Why would he do that for you, for us?'

'You know, it was strange. We had a good chat, actually, probably the first one ever. I told him I didn't want the farm. He said he was sorry, that he hadn't really been in a position to marry again and shouldn't have. He was kind and wished me all the best, as I did him. It was amazing, really.'

Sharif gestured to her to move outside as Mrs Johnson stirred but then resumed her peaceful sleep once more. The old lady's breathing was shallow, but she seemed not to be in any distress. Once out in the quiet corridor, he whispered, 'That all makes sense. Johnson stormed in here today, very agitated, furious, I'd have said, and he took whatever Mrs Johnson had, money, jewellery. When Julianna, the staff nurse, told him that his mother's condition had deteriorated, he basically told her to eff off and stormed out. We've tried calling him several times this evening – she won't last too much longer, I would think – but his phone is switched off. Julia must have taken Bill's threat seriously.'

'Well, the way he spoke to her – I was there –

he wasn't messing around. Bill isn't a man for idle threats. Either way, it's over. Oh, and he said he's not going to be difficult about the divorce. He said just have our solicitor send whatever he needs to sign and he'll do it.'

Sharif drew her into his arms, something he never did within the clinic. 'You're amazing, do you know that? Simply amazing. I can't wait to be married to you.'

'I know.' She grinned, winking at him. 'Now would you like me to sit with Mrs Johnson for a while? You take a break?'

'No, I'm OK. She and I go back a long time. It won't be long now. You can come in with us if you like, or are you exhausted?'

'No, I'm fine. I'll just go and call Joe. He and Luke are out visiting some more McDaids in Reading or somewhere before heading back to Ireland. I texted him from the taxi – he was worried too.'

'I know. I'm so happy and grateful that you managed to solve this. You really should have told me your plan, though...'

'You'd have tried to talk me out of it.' Carmel was matter-of-fact.

'Well, maybe I would, but please, no more solo

runs, OK? We're a team and we make decisions together.'

'Are we having our first fight?' She grinned.

'I hope not, because if today is anything to go by, I'll be on the losing side every time.'

'You might do well to remember that.' She smiled at him and squeezed his hand.

She walked away down the corridor to an alcove with easy chairs and a sofa. She took out her phone, scrolled and pressed call.

'Carmel, so you turned up?'

She could hear the grin in Joe's voice. Briefly, she outlined the events of the day, and both he and Luke were delighted. It sounded like they were having a great time, so she left them to it and returned to Sharif.

Mrs Johnson's breath was very ragged now, and noisy. Sharif had explained to her before that the loosening of mucus in the airways causes what is commonly called the death rattle. Her skin appeared paler too, and her hands were cold. Carmel sat on the other side of the bed from Sharif.

Mrs Johnson seemed a little more agitated than earlier, and Sharif spoke soothingly to her. 'It's all right now, Dorothy, you can go. Everything is all right with the world, everything is fine. Slip away. You're free to go.'

She never opened her eyes but seemed to take a deeper breath and exhaled slowly. Instantly her face became more peaceful; she seemed to release all her pain in that last breath. Sharif sat holding one hand and Carmel the other.

A few moments passed, then Sharif stood and took her pulse and noted the time of death on her chart. Carmel watched him brush her hair back from her face and lean down to kiss her gently on the forehead. 'Thanks for all you did for me, and for this place. Godspeed,' he whispered.

Sharif then notified the morgue team and the all-too-familiar process began.

Quietly, Sharif took Carmel's hand, and together they walked home.

EPILOGUE

The day dawned bright and clear, and Carmel allowed herself to luxuriate in their large bed for a few moments before getting up. It felt strange to sleep alone, but Nadia insisted that she should spend the night before her wedding away from Sharif. He, Joe, Nadia and the rest of the McDaids were staying at a hotel a few miles away.

She switched the alarm off and threw back the covers. The wedding was going to be at noon, and Ivanka was coming to do her hair and make-up. Her dress was so simple, it would be on in a moment. Nadia had helped her choose it, and she was delighted with the ivory raw-silk strapless gown. It was fitted to her waist and then fell to her ankles so gracefully she felt like a princess.

'I think I'm a bit long in the tooth for princess dresses,' she said ruefully when the saleswoman suggested it originally, but at Nadia's insistence, she tried it on. It was perfect on her, and there and then she decided she would wear it. So what if she was forty-one? She'd never dressed up like this before, and she was only doing this once.

Nadia had been so understanding yesterday when Carmel said she wanted to be alone, just to go over to the little chapel and have a talk with her mother. Perhaps it was her Catholic up-bringing and all the time spent in churches, or maybe not, but she felt close to Dolly there. Nadia said Dolly often went there to be alone as well. Carmel wanted to feel that connection before all the excitement started. She'd sat there for an hour yesterday evening and just chatted to her mother, and for Carmel, her mother was there with her. When she came back to the apartment, she found Nadia in the spare room, looking at the photo of Jamilla.

The older woman was embarrassed to have been caught. 'I'm sorry, Carmel dear. This must look awful, like I'm wishing things were different, but I assure you...'

'Nadia, I understand. Jamilla was a huge part of Sharif's life, and of yours and Khalid's as well. Of course she is going to be on your minds today. Please, don't be sorry.' Carmel wanted to reassure this woman who had been so welcoming and kind to her.

They stayed up later than they intended, drinking chai and talking about Jamilla, Khalid and, of course, Dolly, and it was lovely. Seeing the light on as they came off the late shift, Zane and Ivanka called in for a drink to wish her well, and there was lots of good-natured teasing about needing her sleep for the wedding night. Carmel felt embarrassed about that kind of talk around Nadia, but Nadia assured her that she was so happy that Carmel and Sharif were compatible in every way. Carmel had blushed to the roots of her hair at that remark, and Nadia had laughed, that lovely tinkly sound.

Ivanka was an organiser, so she asked Carmel what seemed like twenty questions about her plans for the big day, mentally ticking each thing off as Carmel answered.

'You should have let me get the flamingos. They're not that dear considering that they send an entire flock,' Zane grumbled. His long legs hung over the edge of the sofa.

'Yes, that would be critical all right, a flock of mad exotic birds wandering around,' Carmel said dryly.

'Well, you're a pretty mad and exotic bird yourself,' he joked, and she threw a cushion at him.

'So.' Carmel changed the subject. 'Have you a date?'

Zane sighed theatrically. 'I had, but it turns out he's the flamingo owner and I promised him the gig, and when Sharif flatly refused, he withdrew his favours as it were. Apparently he was finding the whole renting out of bizarre birdlife for functions a tougher business than he first imagined, and he's taking out his disappointment on me. Eating him out of house and home those flamingos are, and nobody wants them.'

'Sorry to hear that,' Carmel sympathised, not daring risking catching Nadia's eye for fear they would both laugh.

'That Tim is going, though, right? Maybe I could become his toy boy. He's quite fit for an old guy and seems nice. And maybe that's what I need, an adoring old man instead of all the cruel young ones.'

Carmel didn't know if he was joking or not. Tim was in his seventies and Zane twenty-five, but anything was possible with her flamboyant friend. Poor Tim would have a heart attack if Zane tried his flirtation tactics on him.

'I think he's still broken-hearted over Brian,' Carmel said diplomatically.

'And he's five decades too old for you – don't be ridiculous,' Ivanka finished, considerably less gently.

'True, but I just want to be adored,' Zane moaned. 'Look at Carmel and Sharif. That's what I want, the way they look at each other. How do I get that? I have to find my Prince Charming or else I'll die in a bedsit in Clapham and the only way the neighbours will know I've died is by the smell. Then they'll get a bunch of gorgeous burly firemen to knock the door down, and they'll find me all decomposing and awful looking.'

Carmel pealed with laughter. 'Well, firstly, I doubt that will happen. You're lovely, so there is someone out there for you. And secondly, for goodness' sake don't take relationship advice from me. I made a right dog's dinner of most of my life up to now. But I think you just have to wait. He's out there, Zane. Someone as fabulous as you won't be alone forever. You just need a little patience.'

'Despite being blessed with good looks, a

sparking personality and shapely calves, patience is not something I have in abundance, darling,' Zane said, easing himself up off the couch. 'Come on Miss Nordic Knickers' – he pulled Ivanka up too – 'let's leave Cinderella here to get ready for her Prince Charming.'

'I'll go too, Carmel. Sleep tight, my darling.' Nadia kissed Carmel's cheek.

Carmel was not used to all the fussing about, so it was with a sigh of relief and a hug of gratitude she let Ivanka, Zane and Nadia out of the apartment that evening. She wanted to gather herself for one last night before the biggest moment of her life.

As she made her way into the shower, there was a knock on the door. She sighed. Much as she loved everyone at Aashna, she hoped it wasn't anyone calling to wish her luck or anything; then she immediately regretted the thought. What she would have done this time last year for some friends, someone to love, a home of her own. She opened the door to a UPS delivery man asking her to sign for a smallish box he proffered.

The box was addressed to Carmel Murphy, a name she hadn't used for years, and she didn't recognise the writing. She took the box to the kitchen, intrigued as to what it might contain.

She opened it with a knife and found a large pink envelope. She lifted the flap and discovered it was an 'On Your Wedding Day' card. Also inside was another box, this one containing a Waterford Crystal large empty photo frame. She opened the card.

To Carmel and Sharif, I wish you all the best on your wedding day. I hope you have a very happy life – you deserve it. The frame is for your wedding photograph.

Best wishes,

Bill

She sat down and stared at the present, incredulous that Bill would have gone to such trouble, but he must have. Julia would never have done it for him, and she seriously doubted either of the girls would. Besides, it was his writing; she recognised it from the dates of herd vaccinations and vet visits that he wrote each month on the calendar on the wall of the kitchen. He'd never written her a card or a letter before, though.

The frame was almost identical to the one she dusted every day on his mantelpiece of him and Gretta, and for a moment, she was transported back to those empty lonely days. She found herself immeasurably touched by the small kindness and felt the tears sting her eyes.

Bill had kept to his word. Julia and Derek Johnson disappeared – the poor lady's horrible son had never even turned up at his mother's funeral – and once the divorce was granted, she wrote to Bill telling him of her wedding plans and thanking him for his cooperation. She'd heard nothing in reply until now. She thanked him quietly and went to get ready. Life really was so strange.

A short while later, she sat alone at her kitchen table, savouring the peaceful solitude. She'd come so far, from a child of the state to the wife of a man incapable of loving her in any sense to here. Nobody could have predicted her life path. For the millionth time, she wished Dolly could have lived to see this day, but it was not to be. She said a prayer for her, and for Brian, and asked them to watch over her and Sharif, today and always.

And then it was time. Ivanka arrived with Nadia in tow, and together they outdid themselves. As Carmel looked in the mirror, she thought, *You look lovely. Not 'not too bad for a kid from an orphanage', or 'passable if you don't notice the flaws', but really, really, lovely,* and she felt proud. She was so happy to marry Sharif. She loved him with all her heart and he loved her. He had given her everything, this beautiful life, but she owed him so much more than that. He gave her the confidence that most kids get from their parents, that sense that she was worthy and precious, and under his love, she grew up.

When Joe arrived, he simply stared at her, beaming. 'Well, my darling girl, you look radiant, absolutely glowing with happiness.'

They walked arm in arm across the lawn to the marquee erected for the wedding. Oscar was a humanist celebrant, so they'd asked him to perform the ceremony, and everyone she loved was gathered inside waiting for her.

'Ready?' Joe smiled down at her and squeezed her arm close to him. She nodded.

All eyes turned to her as she entered the beautifully decorated marquee, and her mother's voice, singing, 'Que sera, sera. Whatever will be, will be. The future's not ours to see. Que sera, sera', recorded at her last-ever party, accompanied Carmel forward to her future.

THE END

I sincerely hope you enjoyed this second book in the Carmel Sheehan Story. The third and final

book, *What Will Be*, is available here: https://geni.
us/WhatWillBeAL

If you would like to hear more from me, and also download a free novel, please go to my website www.jeangrainger.com

Here's a sneak preview of the next book to whet your appetite!

* * *

What Will Be - Chapter 1

CARMEL SAT on the side of the bath trying to breathe normally. Sharif was in the living room watching a documentary about whales, and Nadia was happily surfing the internet on her new tablet. Nadia had decorators in her place, so she was spending a bit more time with Carmel and Sharif to allow the workmen to finish the job quickly. Jen had called Carmel to tell her the exciting news that she was pregnant again. Carmel was thrilled for her sister, of course she was, but why did the news bring stinging tears to her eyes and a pain in the pit of her stomach?

She gazed at her reflection in the mirror over the sink. She looked upset; Sharif would know something was wrong if she came out now. Her naturally blond hair was shiny and sleek, having just been to the hairdresser's today, and she would touch up her makeup, but no matter how she looked, he had a way of seeing past all of it, into her soul.

She'd have to pull herself together. She was forty-one years old, for goodness sake, she'd had her life transformed in ways she could never have imagined, and she a had a home of her own, a loving family, friends, and the love of Sharif, so why on earth was she feeling so despondent? She knew the answer, though she didn't even want to admit it to herself. She wanted a baby.

'Carmel, do you want some tea?' Sharif tapped gently on the bathroom door. The programme must be over.

'Eh, yeah, thanks, I'll be out in a minute,' she called.

'Is everything OK? You've been in there a long time...' She heard the concern in his voice.

'Yes, fine. I'm...reading something on my phone,' she lied, reddening, even though there was nobody to see it. She just wanted him to go away, for a moment or two, to give her a chance to recover.

She tried to keep it together, to not cry.

It was so peculiar, so strong, this longing for a child, and the feeling had taken her totally by surprise. She had never imagined herself as a mother. She'd thought her only chance at motherhood had been her failed attempt with her ex-husband Bill's girls nearly twenty years ago. But even though they were only little when they'd lost their mother to cancer and Carmel and Bill married, the girls had been monopolised by their aunt. There'd been no room for Carmel.

Now that she'd found such happiness with Sharif, she felt frustrated with herself. Why couldn't she just enjoy it? But she couldn't. All she wanted was a child of her own, just one—a boy, a girl, she didn't care.

Being raised in state care in Ireland meant she'd never had a family, never felt part of anything, and now that she was married for love, at long last, things should've been perfect. Sharif was her soul mate, no doubt about it, and his mother Nadia had become almost a surrogate mother to Carmel, as well. Nadia had been best friends with Carmel's birth mother, Dolly, for so long, she was able to bring Dolly alive through her stories. Nadia still felt Dolly's loss keenly, and she sometimes expressed frustration at knowing how close they came to reuniting Dolly with

Carmel. But it wasn't to be. Dolly died months before Sharif finally found Carmel on Facebook. He had promised Dolly he wouldn't give up the search, and he was true to his word. After she died, Nadia and Sharif had helped Carmel in every way imaginable, giving her a life, a home, helping her connect with Joe, her dad, and Jen and Luke, his children. She had so much more than she'd ever imagined she could. They would have done it anyway, even if she and Sharif had not fallen in love, but the fact that they had was a happy coincidence.

The hospice they all ran together, Aashna House, was so busy but such a rewarding place to work, she should have been content. More than content. She should've been doing cartwheels. But here she was crying in the bathroom because her sister, who she'd only known for a year, was pregnant.

Carmel was forty-one and Sharif was forty-six, so they were no spring chickens. He didn't have any children—his first wife had died, and afterwards, once he came out of the cloud of grief, he threw himself into creating Aashna. When he and Carmel had talked about children, ages ago, he seemed to be under the impression that that ship had sailed, and he was mildly regretful but not sad. He was just so grateful and happy to have found love a second time, that was enough. At the time, Carmel said she'd never envisaged herself as a mother, because she was afraid to say what she really wanted. The thoughts swirling around her head at night, as Sharif slept beside her, told her she would probably be hopeless at parenting anyway—she had no experience. What would someone raised in an institution know about being a proper mother? The care workers in Trinity were fine, and even the nuns were all right, but you wouldn't describe any of them as maternal. She wouldn't know where to start to be a mother, she knew that, but nothing would make the yearning disappear.

She was on the pill, and apart from that one conversation with Sharif, the subject was never raised again.

Something had come over his face that day they talked about kids, something she couldn't read, and she was afraid to pry. After all, he'd plucked her from her miserable marriage and delivered letters from Dolly, who had spent her life looking for her only child, to no avail. Apparently, the loss of her daughter was the heartache of her life and the years spent searching and getting nowhere meant she'd died unfulfilled. The thought of it all made Carmel happy and sad in equal measure. She would have loved to meet her and regretted deeply the fact that her mother was unable to find her, but the knowledge that she hadn't been abandoned as a child, discarded like something unwanted, served to heal some of the broken bits inside her.

She took a deep breath and tried to bring herself back to the present. She needed to pull herself together. She was afraid Sharif would think she wasn't happy, or that she was ungrateful. She knew deep down he would think none of those things, but the insecurities she carried, deeply ingrained by twenty years of state care, followed by seventeen years of an empty, cold marriage, were not easily erased.

Before she went back out, she took one more look at herself in the mirror over the sink. The strong spot lighting, ideal for putting on makeup or shaving, hid nothing, and the pain was there in her eyes. Both Sharif and Nadia were very perceptive; she'd have to do a better job of acting like everything was fine.

'Chai or Barry's?' Sharif asked as she emerged.

She smiled. 'Chai, please.' He handed her a cup of chai, which she'd initially found revolting. At first, she'd been afraid to say she hated it, because

Sharif never drank normal black tea, even though he wouldn't have cared if she did. But after almost a year of living with him, she'd actually come to like chai.

'Are you sure you're OK?' He put his head to one side, his brown eyes looking intently at her.

'Honestly, I'm fine.' She smiled and kissed his cheek. 'Thanks for the tea.' She sipped it.

'Does it still taste like boiled weeds?' He grinned, teasing her about a remark he'd overheard her make to her sister Jennifer on the phone months previously. The very next day, he'd gone out and bought her a big box of Barry's tea bags from Ireland.

'Well, aromatic weeds, I'll go that far.'

'So how's Jen?' he asked.

'Good, she's fine. Joe is doing a job for them in the house, and Luke has a new girlfriend, it seems.' She didn't tell him about the pregnancy; she just couldn't get the words out. She was spared further elaboration when Sharif's beeper went. He was needed in the hospice. He glanced at it and kissed her cheek. 'I've to go. I don't know how long I'll be, but text if you need me, OK?'

'Sure.' She hugged him. He was so muscular

and smelled of sandalwood and soap. She felt a familiar stirring of attraction.

Something in her embrace caused him to pause and give her a slow smile. 'Mmm, you're so gorgeous. I'll try to be back before you go to bed.' He murmured it all so his mother didn't hear.

'I'll wait up,' she whispered back.

Nadia was so deep in a very animated FaceTime chat in her native Urdu with one of her relatives in Karachi that she wouldn't have heard them even if they spoke normally. Likewise, Carmel hadn't the faintest idea what Nadia was saying. Sharif could speak Urdu too, as it was the language of their home as he grew up. Carmel sometimes felt bad that they had to speak English around her all the time, so as not to exclude her, but they assured her they were equally comfortable in both languages.

She slipped into their bedroom, leaving Nadia to chat, relieved to be alone. Something made her pick up the phone and call her dad. The discovery that Joe even existed was still new, but in many ways, she felt as if she'd known him all her life. They spoke every day, sometimes several times a day, on the phone. Sometimes just for a minute or two. She knew he wasn't a phone chatter, but he seemed to understand that she needed to have that connection, and to make her feel less needy, he called her as much as she called him.

'Hi, darling, how are you?' he answered on the first ring, his strong Dublin accent immediately soothing her troubled soul.

'I'm OK. You?' She tried to inject some enthusiasm into her voice. She wished he was here in London; she could've really used one of his bear hugs.

'Grand out, pet, flying it. Your cousin Aisling's wedding is taking up everyone's time here. I'm telling you, there was fellas put on the moon with less organisation. I'm staying out of it all as much as I can, but she just rang and asked me to make a sweet cart or something. I thought she was losing her marbles, like sweets like a child would have, at the wedding reception, only there's no kids going. And I sez to her, Aisling, pet, when people are drinking pints and glasses of wine or whatever, the last thing on their minds are fizzy jellies or smarties or whatever, but she wasn't having a bar of it. Tis all the go now, apparently. Sweets, did you ever hear the like? So off with mad old uncle Joe to the hardware place tomorrow to get the stuff for it. I don't know, more money than sense...'

Carmel chuckled. She loved to hear the stories

of the extended McDaid tribe.

'Now, yourself and Sharif and Nadia are still on for the trip, aren't ye? I've a great itinerary set up. Come here to me now, you're the very woman for this job. I was talking to Tim earlier, and he was saying he didn't think he'd be able to make it, and I didn't like to pry. I know he has some things to sort out over in Mayo with his parents' land and everything, but he was all up for the trip the last time we spoke, and now he's backing out. Could you talk to him? See what's going on? He and Brian were very private about their relationship and everything—well, they had to be, on account of Tim's family—and I know Brian was my brother and we were close and everything, but I just don't feel comfortable pressing Tim.

'There's something up though, I know it, so maybe you could get it out of him? He trusts you. I think it would do him good to come over; it's been decades since he set foot in his native country, and I think it would be to his benefit to lay a few ghosts to rest. Anyway, it's his choice, but ye can fly into Dublin, and we can all rent the minibus and take off for the West of Ireland, have a proper holiday, not just a weekend for the wedding. Jen, Damien, and the baby, and

Luke are coming as well, so we'll have great craic.'

'Yes, we've the flights booked and everything. Though I can't say I'm looking forward to being back.' Carmel loved that she could be so honest with Joe. Their relationship had started out that way and had continued, no pretence, no saying what she thought he wanted to hear. It was such a departure for her after a lifetime of watching what she said, trying to please, to fit in. 'I'm excited to go to Aisling's wedding, of course, but I just feel happier out of Ireland, you know? Like I escaped. And I'm scared to go back in case I get sucked back in or something. Stupid, I know...'

'Ah, 'tisn't one bit stupid, my love, not a bit of it. But as I'm always telling you, the reason your experience here was so bad, so empty, was because of the behaviours of a few people, not the whole country. You're Irish, Carmel, your mam was Irish, and so am I, and no matter what, this place is in your bones. It wouldn't do you any good to build up a big wall between you and it. Like, Sharif is Pakistani, he doesn't live there or anything, but he knows who he is and where he comes from. That's important to the human spirit. I think it is, anyway.'

'Maybe you're right. I'm trying just to see it as

a holiday, but do me a favour? Keep me away from Ballyshanley, County Offaly, OK?' She smiled.

'Well, I have no notion of going near any town that is home to your ex and his mad witch of a sister, so yes, we're staying out of that part of the country entirely, just in case. But wait till you see where I am taking ye, you're going to love it. We need to spend a few days in Westport, to let Tim get things sorted legally with his family farm and all of that, provided of course that you can convince him to come. I'm going to show you all the places I wish I'd been able to show you when you were small, when I could have been a proper dad to you.'

Though his words were tinged with sadness at all the time that was lost, his enthusiasm was infectious, and she felt her mood lighten. 'You're a proper dad now,' she said quietly. 'And I'm so glad to have you.'

'We've a lot of making up to do, Carmel, a lot. Please God we'll have lots of years together. I used to think my job was done, and after June died, I was very low. Jen and Luke were reared and doing grand, so I felt like I was only filling in time, but now that you're in my life, I feel like I want to live for years and years to try to make up for all the time lost.'

Carmel felt a rush of love for this man, her dad. She used to dream about her parents, when she was small, but she couldn't have dreamed up a better man than Joe McDaid.

'You will. Sure you're fit as a trout, as Sister Kevin used to say. Actually, Sharif was saying the other day he was at a conference and there's a new drug for the treatment of asthma in trial that is having great effects, so we might both be even healthier in the future.'

'Imagine that.' Joe chuckled.

'Oh, and I'll ring Tim tomorrow, invite him for lunch,' Carmel promised. 'He's finding the days long without Brian, and Christmas was so lonely for him. He doesn't go to his daughter or his son, but I've never raised the question with him. As you said, he's very private, but I'll do my best. I can't think why they are estranged; they could be such a comfort to him now that Brian is gone. It seems such a waste.'

'I know, the poor man. He gave his whole life to my brother, they had a long and happy marriage, even though the state would never recognise it as such, but that's what it was, and his heart is broken, I can hear it in his voice. No wonder himself and his children aren't close. If I had to keep something as big as that—the pain at losing the only person I ever loved—from Luke and Jen and you, I wouldn't be close to ye either. The only reason people are close is because they trust each other. If there's no trust, then there can't be anything else either.'

Carmel loved it when he said things like that. As if she was as valid as the son and daughter he'd reared from infancy.

'I know. Maybe he just can't go there now, after all this time. Who knows? I mean, his children must be in their fifties by now; he was only married for a short time when he was very young. I'll try to bring it up with him anyway, or at least figure out why he's backing out.'

'Sure that's all you can do.'

'Well, we're going to be a right motley crew on this bus trip you've planned, but we'll have a laugh, I'm sure.'

'We sure will. Now, pet, I'm going to have to love you and leave you, there's a meeting in the parish hall about trying to do something about the homelessness situation. It's awful, you know, families living in hotels and the whole city full of empty properties. I'm volunteering to get them into habitable shape.'

'Sure, you are a marvel, you do know that? Give me a call tomorrow if you get a chance.'

'Will do, pet, night night.'

Carmel ended the call and realised that talking to her dad had made her feel better. She wondered if she ever might confide in him about her baby dreams. She doubted it. Despite all the love and family and everything she'd been gifted with, she still felt separate and alone sometimes.

Chapter 2

'IT IS QUITE IMPOSSIBLE. I mean, honestly, what am I going to do?' Nadia was fuming as she paced around Carmel and Sharif's kitchen the next day. 'I didn't even invite her, and she just announced she was coming. Booked flights and everything without a word! Who does that? I can't have her! She will drive me insane...'

'Maybe it won't be so bad. After all, her husband isn't long dead; maybe she just needs to spend some time with her sister...' Carmel was trying to be supportive; she knew how much Nadia's sister Zeinab irritated her.

'And what about our trip to Ireland? Her so-called visit is right in the middle of it. It is as if she knew the very worst time and picked it on purpose.'

Carmel tried to suppress a smile as Sharif grinned behind his newspaper.

'She could come with us,' Carmel suggested. 'I'm sure Joe won't mind.' Sharif winked at Carmel—he knew how her suggestion would go down with his mother.

'Come? Come to Ireland? Have you lost your mind? All of us stuck in a little bus with Zeinab and her ailments and her complaining and her snobbery? It would be hell, absolute hell. No, I'll just have to cancel, there's no other way.' Nadia was devastated. Carmel knew how much she was looking forward to the trip. She and Joe got along so well, and at one stage, Carmel had even though there might have been a spark of romance there —but no, they just really had fun together.

'She will come over here, and complain, and criticise, and tell me how my house is too small, my bottom is too big, my *gajar ka halwa* is too dry —I can't bear it. There is a reason I live five thousand miles from my older sister.' Nadia's tiny frame was almost quivering with frustration. Her normally serene brown eyes glittered.

Sharif sighed and put down the paper. He stood, resting his hands on his mother's shoulders. His six-foot-two bulk dwarfed her. 'Ammi, you're making this worse by getting yourself into such a state. If you won't contact her and say not to come, which you are perfectly entitled to do, by the way, then you'll have to come up with a way of not letting her get under your skin. You have to come to Ireland; you've been looking forward to it and now it's all set up. Carmel's right. We'll just take her with us. I think Zeinab might actually enjoy Ireland, and she'll have Joe, me, Tim, Luke and Damien, not to mention little Sean to fawn over. You always said she's an old flirt and behaves much better around men, so maybe it's the best idea.'

Carmel smiled as Nadia managed to calm down. Sharif had that effect on people. Somehow, he managed to make people realise that nothing was ever as bad as it seemed. Nadia sighed and relaxed a little.

'Ah, Sharif, why does she do this? Always the same. Remember the time she came over to help when your father was ill? Dolly and she nearly came to blows, and I was so stressed, trying to keep her away from poor Khalid. The man was dying, and still on and on she would talk, jabbering away incessantly about people we don't know, always this one and that one from Karachi society. It was all to show off how well connected she and Tariq were, as if Khalid gave a hoot about that... Even if we did ask her to come to Ireland with us, she would find some reason not to. She would refuse simply because she would know I want to go.'

Carmel was so fond of her mother-in-law, she hated to see her so wound up. Sharif adored his mother, too, but sometimes thought she was inclined to be a bit melodramatic. She was just a really animated person, the kind who talked with her hands and told great stories. Carmel, after years of people being guarded and detached with her, loved Nadia's spontaneity and how she wore her heart on her sleeve. Which gave Carmel an idea. 'Look, why doesn't Sharif call her? He can explain that we're all planning a trip to Ireland, about my cousin's wedding and all of that, and how we can't change it at this stage so if she wants to visit then she'll have to come to Ireland with us. You said yourself she idolises Sharif, and she'd never refuse him anything.'

Carmel tried to quell her own anxiety. Confrontation and outbursts of emotion unsettled her, though she was trying to learn that they were a normal part of human interaction. Since she'd never experienced it in her life before, sometimes normal family interactions confused her. Once, when her friend Zane had described an argument he'd had with his sister one Friday, Carmel had been horrified and really worried about him all weekend. But when he came back to work on Monday, he was full of how he and his sister had had such a laugh at a wine tasting on Sunday. And the first time Carmel had had an argument with Sharif, over something silly, she'd convinced herself the relationship was over. But he'd come home, and they'd talked and solved it.

Carmel had even confided her fears to him, and he'd explained that people who loved each other sometimes fell out—it was no big deal. She was trying to be more relaxed about conflict, along with about a million other life adjustments she had to make every day.

But Nadia seemed genuinely distressed at the prospect of her sister's arrival. Maybe the trip to Ireland wasn't such a good idea after all. Carmel didn't really want to go back, Tim was backing out as well, and now Zeinab was arriving.

The holiday had been mooted as an idea by Joe last summer, before she and Sharif were married, as a way of helping Tim go back to Mayo and sort out his family affairs, as well as giving

Carmel some time with family and to see the sights of her country she'd never seen before.

Carmel wondered why Tim was suddenly reluctant. He'd told her his story briefly, how as a young man, he had been found kissing one of the local lads in the barn by his father and was told to get out and never come back. The man never again wanted to see his son. Tim had taken his father at his word and had only returned once since the old man died, for his mother's funeral. Tim moved to England and married in London, as was expected, but of course, the marriage was a disaster. So one day his wife confronted him with her suspicions and left, taking their little son and daughter with her. Tim met Joe's brother, Brian—or perhaps he knew him before the marriage broke up, Carmel never asked—and they'd lived happily and quietly together until Brian's death last year.

The idea of going back to Ireland, even with Sharif and all of her new family, made Carmel nauseous, so maybe Tim felt the same. She was convinced there was nothing there for her anymore. The shy, insecure, lonely woman she was still lurked inside somewhere, but she was stronger now than she could have ever imagined.

A big part of her believed that strength would disappear the minute she set foot on Irish soil.

'Carmel is right,' Nadia said with a sigh. 'Perhaps if you speak to her, Sharif... She is not so difficult with you...'

Sharif gave his mother a squeeze with one arm. 'That's the spirit. It will be fine—I'll call her this afternoon and smooth it all over. Now, don't you have to meet with the family of Juliette Binchet?'

Nadia glanced at her watch. 'Yes, and I'm late. She was a difficult woman too, and her daughter and son are now at loggerheads about the funeral, mainly because the daughter wants a very flashy affair to show off to her friends and he doesn't want to spend the money.'

Carmel smiled at Nadia. 'You'll sort everything out beautifully to everyone's satisfaction, like you always do.'

'We'll see. These two would try the patience of a saint, as Dolly used to say. Anyway, see you two later.' She gave them each a quick kiss on the cheek and was gone.

Once they were alone, Sharif put his arms around Carmel, his eyes searching her face. She loved how his eyes crinkled up when he smiled.

'OK, I've tried waiting for you to tell me

what's wrong, but you won't, so I see I'm going to have to extract it.'

He led her to the courtyard of their apartment. The plants she had sown last summer, when she arrived, were blooming in profusion, and the fragrance of the lilac and sweet pea was heady.

'If we have to sit here till tonight, I want to know what's up. You've been distracted for the last few days, and sometimes I watch you and you're a million miles away and, judging by the look on your face, it's not somewhere pleasant, so I'm worried.' His voice was soothing and gentle as always. 'Remember, we agreed—no secrets, no keeping things in, we say what we feel.'

Carmel sighed. 'OK... I don't want to go to Ireland.'

'OK.' He paused. 'The first thing is you're a grown adult...'

'I know, I know...' She finished his mantra: 'I'm a grown adult who can make her own decisions.'

For her first forty years, she'd never had any autonomy. Everyone else had decided what would happen, and she was expected to fall in with it. Sharif was gradually trying to give her back that independence.

'But my dad has gone to so much trouble, and

he loves Ireland so much, and he hates that I just don't feel the same way about the place. If I back out, I'd feel like I was letting him down—I *would* be letting him down—and they've all done so much, been so welcoming, especially considering a year ago he didn't even know I existed.

'I know it's not too much to ask to go on a little holiday with my family. And, of course, the wedding, it will be the first time I meet all these cousins and aunts and uncles, and I know he's dying for me to meet them. I longed for a family for most of my life, but it just all feels...I don't know, overwhelming? And then there's Tim; he's getting cold feet as well, apparently, for different reasons maybe—I don't know. I told Dad I'd speak to him. And now Nadia needs some way to cope with your auntie, which is a further complication, and to be honest, I'm happier here than I've ever been anywhere, and I just don't want to go back.'

'All right, now tell me exactly why you hate the thought of it so much.' Sharif held her hand, making small circles on her palm with his thumb, which she found strangely relaxing.

Carmel thought for a moment. 'Because I think—and I know this is mad—but I'm afraid I'll be that person, the woman I was when you met me first, if I go back. My independence, the courage I've got, is all to do with moving away from all of that, and going back, well, it feels...terrifying, if I'm honest. Back there, I didn't know about my mother, my father, nothing. I was nobody.' She tried to keep the tremor out of her voice. 'Here, in Aashna, I'm not nobody. I'm Carmel the events manager, Carmel the friend, Carmel the daughter. Here, I'm your wife. Things I never dreamed I could be.

He drew her into his arms and held her tight. 'What would Dolly say?'

Carmel didn't answer.

'I'll tell you, shall I?' He took her phone from her pocket, scrolled to her videos, and selected the one of Dolly's last birthday party, in Aashna, a few months before she died. Carmel watched the video every day.

There her mother was, in a wheelchair, wearing a blue dress and red lipstick, and a birthday girl hat. She sang in her unmistakable Dublin accent:

'When I was just a little girl, I asked my mother, what will I be? Will I be handsome? Will I be rich? Here's what she said to me. Que sera, sera, whatever will be will be. The future's not ours to see, que sera, sera.'

Sharif paused the video before Dolly gave her speech, and looked down into Carmel's eyes.

'When *you* were a little girl, she moved heaven and earth to find you, but your grandfather made sure she never could. If she was here now, she'd say, "What will be, will be, Carmel, my love, but go forward, face the future with bravery." You are one of the bravest people I've ever met, and I know it must be scary, but you're a different person now, you're stronger, and you can do this. You might even enjoy it. But in this, just like everything else, we're a team. If you decide you can't or you really don't want to go, then I've got your back, 100 percent. Always.'

She thought about bringing up the other thing, the pregnancy or lack of it, but didn't. 'Thanks. I know you have, and I really appreciate it. It'll be fine, I suppose, and I'll have everyone with me, and Joe assures me we're not going near Ballyshanley, County Offaly.'

'I don't know, maybe Julia would invite us all for tea?' Sharif teased.

'Unless you wanted it laced with arsenic, I wouldn't be drinking anything she made you.' Carmel didn't need to remind him of the lengths her ex-husband's sister was willing to go to hurt them. She'd tried to destroy Aashna last year, colluding with a criminal to bring a malpractice suit against Sharif. In the end, Carmel had had to visit Bill in Ballyshanley to get him to call her off. Carmel swore she would never go back to Ireland that day—the day she left Bill and the lonely farm for good—and yet here she was, making plans to return to the country of her birth.

To CONTINUE READING this book - click this link. https://geni.us/WhatWillBeAL

AFTERWORD

This book came about, like most of my books, by
chance. I was driving home one day when a
woman called a radio talk show here in Ireland.
The discussion that day was on the harrowing
subject of the treatment of women and children
in the institutions set up by the Catholic Church
with the tacit approval of the Irish state between
he years 1920 and 1990.

In a time of strict censure on how morality
was perceived, women who became pregnant
outside of marriage were systematically and cru-
elly imprisoned in places where they were expected to do hard manual labour for the duration
of their pregnancy, for which they received no
pay. Women and girls who were victims of sexual

crime, incest or rape, had no recourse to the law. In fact, if they tried to leave these places they were returned by the Irish police, though they had committed no crime. Once their child was born, almost always without access to any pain relief, the children were adopted without the mother's consent. Needless to mention, the fathers of these children are never mentioned in the narrative, it was as if the women conceived all on their own.

It was a dark and awful time in our history and we need, as a nation to stand up and face it.

This woman on the radio that day was one such child and she spoke of her life in an institution. She was at pains to point out that while she didn't suffer the abuses we have come to expect from such places, she was neglected in the sense that nobody loved her. She was made to feel that she was a burden, a person who was a drain on the state. She described being raised without the love of parents, the companionship of siblings. She explained that nobody had ever taught her how to drive, do laundry, cook, how to buy a train ticket. The things our children pick up just by simply being part of a family, were a mystery to her. She spoke so eloquently about being thrown out into the world at eighteen, with nobody to help her and no idea how to exist. She described it as being as if everyone else had been to a school on how to live but she never went and so felt entirely adrift.

She had imagined what living in a family would be like, based on TV programmes, and had rushed into a marriage without the first person who offered, in the hope that finally she would belong somewhere. Unsurprisingly, it didn't work out.

I had to pull over and listen to her story, so touched was I by what she had to say.

Quite rightly, those innocent children and women who suffered so horrendously at the hands of people purporting to be doing the work of God must be heard and cared for and some effort made to lessen the pain, but this woman will never be part of that system. She wasn't a sex abuse victim, she wasn't forced into slave labour, she wasn't beaten, but she was not loved, or cared for or prepared for the adult world and that too is so very wrong.

That night the character of Carmel was born, and I hope I have managed to do that dark time justice.

ABOUT THE AUTHOR

Jean Grainger is a USA Today bestselling Irish author. She writes historical and contemporary Irish fiction and her work has very flatteringly been compared to the late great Maeve Binchy.

She lives in a stone cottage in Cork with her husband Diarmuid and the youngest two of her four children. The older two are finally self sufficient, productive members of society. There are a variety of animals there too, all led by two cute but clueless micro-dogs called Scrappy and Scoobi.

f

ALSO BY JEAN GRAINGER

To get a free novel and to join my readers club (100% free and always will be)

Go to www.jeangrainger.com

The Tour Series

The Tour

Safe at the Edge of the World

The Story of Grenville King

The Homecoming of Bubbles O'Leary

Finding Billie Romano

Kayla's Trick

The Carmel Sheehan Story

Letters of Freedom

The Future's Not Ours To See

What Will Be

The Robinswood Story

What Once Was True

Return To Robinswood

Trials and Tribulations

The Star and the Shamrock Series

The Star and the Shamrock

The Emerald Horizon

The Hard Way Home

The World Starts Anew

The Queenstown Series

Last Port of Call

The West's Awake

The Harp and the Rose

Roaring Liberty

Standalone Books

So Much Owed

Shadow of a Century

Under Heaven's Shining Stars

Catriona's War

Sisters of the Southern Cross

Made in the USA
Middletown, DE
07 October 2023

40413887R00205